Till Tomorrow Never Comes

A W Anthony

Contents

1. The End   1
2. The Story Begins   21
3. August 1974   30
4. September 1974   55
5. October 1974   73
6. November 1974   95
7. December 1974   105
8. 1975 Begins   122
9. The Long Summer   139
10. The Plan   144
11. Regrouping   160
12. Getting On With Life   171
13. The Thunderbolt   197
14. Till Tomorrow Isn't Coming   210

Chapter 1
The End

Getting the Long Face

K urt Kellerman sat in the doctor's office with his thirty-year-old daughter, Jennifer. The white-haired, sixty-five-year-old Kurt, with the nervous habits of a lifetime, kept yawning and sighing. His hair was straight, short, and without body. At five-ten and well over two hundred twenty pounds, he was overweight. The first thing you noticed when you looked at Kurt were bright blue eyes that twinkled like a mischievous little boy's. His daughter had the same bright blue eyes as her father. She kept tapping on her cell phone. Both were bouncing their legs up and down. Except for her long brown hair, she looked like a younger, healthier version of her father.

Finally, Dr. Ashraf entered and sat down. In a calm, professional manner, he said, "You have Stage 3 pancreatic cancer. Your tests show that it has spread from your pancreas to several lymph nodes." He had a sympathetic smile, dark brown eyes, a dark complexion, and closely cropped black hair.

"Is it terminal?" Kurt remembered an old western, *McLintock,*

with John Wayne, where a character described his doctor giving
him a terminal diagnosis as giving him "the long face." It
described the moment accurately.

Dr. Ashraf looked at his computer screen. He scrolled down
and looked at some images and reports. "Probably. With your
permission, I would like to start chemotherapy as soon as possible. Hopefully, we can slow the growth of the cancer. There are
no guarantees; much depends on how well your body responds
to the treatments."

Jennifer spoke up. "How long are we talking about when you
say 'probably' terminal?"

"The average patient, with these conditions, will live
between six and seven months. If the chemotherapy works, you
could have longer. Eighty-four percent of patients die within
three-and-a-half years."

"Schedule the treatments as quickly as possible. I'm ready,
Doctor." *It's more or less what I expected. Somehow, this doesn't seem
real, but then, I'm ready to die.* Kurt turned to his daughter and
asked if she had any other questions. She didn't.

They went home and shared the news with the rest of the
family. Everyone knew there would be bad news that day, but
hearing it spoken seemed unreal. It was true, yet it felt like a
bad dream.

Meghan, Kurt's wife, tried to be strong, but tears were
streaming down her cheeks. When she saw that Kurt was
handling it well, she went to her room for a few minutes. When
she came back, her green eyes were red from crying. She
clutched a handkerchief in her hand. At sixty-one, she was a few
years younger than Kurt. Her hair was still dark brown like her
daughter's, but wisps of gray were beginning to appear. Meghan
was five foot six and weighed one hundred twenty pounds. She
looked young for her age, except for those annoying wisps of
gray.

She'd worried about Kurt for months but didn't want to believe this diagnosis was accurate. Meghan was scared. She had always been an introvert. Kurt was the only person who had ever been able to draw her out. She couldn't imagine life without him. Her mind whirled, but she knew she needed to return to the family room and be with her husband and children.

As she walked back through the house, she looked with pride at her decorating. Everything was neat and in place. There wasn't any dust. Not a single picture was crooked. Her home was neat, clean, and orderly. Meghan loved her house. She and Kurt had bought it and worked together to improve it.

John, Kurt and Meghan's oldest son, received the news stoically. He'd just gotten home from Chicago a few days earlier. John tried to look on the bright side of things, but it was hard to know what he thought.

"It sounds like you've got a correct diagnosis, so that's good. New treatments and medications are discovered every day. I think you've just got to fight this thing, and it will work out, Pops."

John looked a great deal like his mother. At six foot two, one hundred seventy pounds, he looked like an athlete. His hair was the same full-bodied, dark brown hair as his mother's. But like his siblings, he had his father's bright blue eyes.

Kurt left the room for a few minutes. He came back with a smile on his face. He seemed composed. *I've got to make this as easy on them as possible.*

James was the middle child. He'd been with his parents for the last week. James accompanied his father to his first appointment with Dr. Ashraf. James looked a great deal like his father, only taller. James was six-three, weighed two hundred thirty pounds, and was prematurely gray. He had the same eyes, smile, and nose. He alone suspected the correct diagnosis.

When James was alone with John and Jennifer, he'd shared his suspicions. "Dad shouldn't have wasted time with those quacks." A man he'd known in Fort Wayne had the same symptoms as his father the previous year. That man was already dead.

In many ways, James had already accepted the news weeks before they heard it from the doctor. James didn't shed any tears, at least not now. He was very much a realist.

Jennifer shared her fears with her brothers. "I've got to stay here and support them. They depend on me. The two of you live too far away. This is all on me."

Jennifer was doing her best to hold up for her mom and dad. She wanted to get away so she could process it. She lived just a few miles away. While John was talking, her mother was crying in the bedroom, and James was sitting in silence. Jennifer came over and offered to do things for her father.

"Can I get you something to drink? Is there anything I can do for you?" She kept looking for something to do.

When Meghan returned to the room, John immediately hugged his mother. The two of them seemed to know what the other was thinking. Both were struggling to accept the news. They knew Kurt was sick, but the idea that he was terminal was unacceptable to them.

Kurt realized what Jennifer was going through. She wanted to help in some tangible way. "Princess, could you get me a Coke? I could use a nice cold drink."

She nearly ran to the kitchen to get it. She returned with a large glass filled with ice and Coke and sat it on the end table by her father.

"Thank you. You've been a big help today, Jennifer. You've all been a big help to me." Kurt got up and hugged Meghan.

Two or three of them spoke at the same time. "What are we going to do?"

"I will start the chemotherapy and any other treatments Dr. Ashraf suggests. You can help by praying and helping one another. It can't get much worse than it's been for the past six months, so we'll take it one day at a time."

Phone calls were made to those who needed to know. But terminal illness is something for the immediate family and the closest of friends to face. It wasn't something that Kurt Kellerman wanted to advertise.

While the children were making calls, Meghan went into Kurt's office. His desk was a mess. She was going to dust it. Instead, she picked up scattered papers and started rearranging and stacking them. She straightened up a few pictures and other items that were always there. Some pens, rubber bands, and paper clips were put into the proper drawers. Meghan liked things to be orderly. It gave her a sense of comfort. Kurt's messy desk stressed her to no end.

After that, she joined the others and talked with the rest of the family about dinner. She needed to be busy doing something. She needed to mother her children and take care of her husband.

Only two weeks ago, Dr. Clappenham, from another clinic, had told Kurt that he didn't know what Kurt's problem was, but the good news was that he was cancer-free. No one in the family believed Clappenham had a clue. Several had been urging Kurt to go to a different clinic and see almost anyone else. Now he had a doctor who seemed to know what he was doing.

During a Caribbean cruise in early April, Kurt had come down with a cold. He got tired walking around the cruise ports; his leg hurt, and he needed more sleep than usual. When he got home, he didn't get better. It just seemed like some bug that people get when they travel. Then he injured his leg while helping someone move some furniture. The leg took what seemed like forever to heal.

Then he noticed his ankle swelled. Of course, this wasn't anything new. He sprained his ankle twice while playing high school football; Kurt's ankles sometimes puffed up overnight.

When he looked at it, he realized it wasn't just the ankle. The swelling went all the way up to the knee and higher. For the first time in years, he voluntarily went to the doctor.

Could it be congestive heart failure? Dad, Grandpa, and Great-Uncle Frank all had it before dying of heart attacks and strokes. I'm probably overreacting, but it won't hurt to make sure. The doctor ordered some labs and said it didn't look like anything too serious. This calmed Kurt down a little, and he went back to work.

Two hours later, he got a call. It was the doctor's nurse. "Go to the hospital immediately. Don't go anywhere else or do anything else. You need some testing done as soon as possible."

Dropping everything, Kurt drove to the hospital. *The nurse sounded serious. She was probably overreacting. It surely wasn't anything that bad, but why did she rush me to the hospital?* When he arrived, he went to the desk and was sent to an intake counselor. He sat down in a room full of people who were waiting and looked very bored. The man next to Kurt complained about the wait. It was annoying.

When Dad died, another patient started yelling when the doctors walked out on him to try and save Dad. He kept shouting, "I was here first."

Kurt looked at him. "Hey! This is where it's good news if you must wait. What's bad is when you're at the hospital and someone comes out and tells you that your condition is so serious and so dangerous that you have been moved to the top of the stack. You never want to be the person at the hospital whose situation is so serious that you get to cut."

No sooner were the words out of Kurt's mouth than an intake counselor walked into the room and called his name. His file was marked STAT. He was to go to radiology and not leave the hospital after an ultrasound until the doctor approved his release. The blood work indicated that a deep vein thrombosis was likely. However, the ultrasound was negative. They released Kurt and sent him home.

Over the next few weeks, he began to have diarrhea. The swelling was worse, too, and now affected both legs to his waist. His back hurt, and he'd never had back problems. Kurt could only wear gym shorts, flip-flops, and T-shirts. Anything else was just too painful on his lower body. It just became his new routine. Another trip to the hospital revealed a blood clot and deep vein thrombosis. But this still didn't explain all of Kurt's symptoms.

Kurt was getting frustrated. *Something is wrong. I'm seeing four different doctors, and nothing is better. Instead, I'm getting worse. How is physical therapy going to take care of my bowels and bladder? This is ridiculous.*

His son-in-law stopped by and offered to drive him to St. Louis to see if a doctor there could get better results. Kurt didn't feel like riding for two hours, as sitting in the car was painful.

Nothing got better. One doctor sent him to physical therapy; another ordered a colonoscopy. Kurt had X-rays, CT scans, and a couple of exploratory surgeries, but his condition continued to deteriorate. He began to lose hope. Kurt drove to the physical therapy office to cancel his appointments.

"I'm sorry. You've been great, but this doesn't help. I've been going to the doctor for nearly four months. I've been coming here for two months. For the first time since this all started, I've hit bottom. I feel like I'm dying, and no one is doing anything." He paused for a moment. "I'm sorry, I shouldn't be telling you. I should be telling my doctors. I've tried to be optimistic, but I've reached that point where I'm ready to give up. Thanks again for trying to help. But cancel the rest of my appointments."

Dr. Clappenham did a surgical biopsy on a lymph node. When he received the pathology report, he had Kurt come into his office. The doctor assured Kurt that whatever was going on, he was cancer-free. Kurt realized he had to go to a different doctor at a different clinic.

He asked his family physician for a referral. She referred Kurt to see Dr. Ashraf, a medical oncologist. The appointment was in three days. Dr. Ashraf ordered blood work, a CT scan, and a potential image-guided needle biopsy.

Kurt went online and looked up his symptoms. He also looked up the treatments Dr. Ashraf ordered. It was clear that Dr. Ashraf believed there was cancer somewhere. The fact that nearly six months had been wasted meant the cancer had plenty of time to spread and grow. Kurt didn't say anything to anyone in the family. But considering how miserable he felt and the things Dr. Ashraf ordered, he expected bad news.

Ten days later, Kurt and Jennifer went to Dr. Ashraf's office. The test results were back. Six months of questions, deterioration, and wasted time had passed. But now, armed with what Kurt believed to be a competent doctor and an accurate diagnosis, he was ready to move forward.

Eight days later, Kurt received his first chemotherapy treatment. He tolerated it well. It upset his bowels and stomach, but they had been a train wreck for several months already. *What's the difference?* The swelling in his legs and feet started going down. Within a few weeks, he could wear sweatpants and shoes if they were two sizes too large. That wasn't great, but it was an improvement over his previous outfits. This was good news, with winter coming.

Dr. Ashraf came in at Kurt's third appointment. "I'm afraid the prognosis is not encouraging. The treatment has reduced some of the tumors in your lymph nodes, so your swelling is down. Unfortunately, it appears to have spread to the lining of your abdominal cavity."

"That's all right. I have confidence in you. I'm ready for whatever happens, and I'm not afraid."

Kurt wasn't worried. He had a competent doctor, a loving family, some wonderful friends, and a deep faith in God with which to face what was coming. Kurt accepted the doctor's statistical probabilities as the ones he should plan for.

A couple from their church stopped by the following week. The wife tried to encourage Kurt and Meghan. "God is the Great Physician. I believe he's going to heal Kurt. You shouldn't be talking about dying."

Her husband joined in. "Amen."

After they left, Kurt was irritated. *Why don't they take it seriously that I'm probably going to die? I wish they would keep quiet instead of pretending everything will be fine.*

Meghan asked, "What's wrong?"

"Why can't people accept that I'm dying? They want to pretend that no one ever dies. I know God works miracles, but I don't see any reason to believe that will happen in my case."

"They were just trying to give you hope. They tried to be caring and kind."

"But they ignore the facts! Everyone dies sooner or later. The sooner we accept that I'm probably going to die and soon, the better prepared we'll be when it happens!" Kurt smiled at Meghan, who was upset about his outburst. "But if I mess up Dr. Ashraf's calculations and live a long time, we'll have a big party and celebrate. Okay?" Kurt smiled his boyish smile at Meghan again.

Meghan smiled back. Kurt realized this was much harder on her than it was on him. He needed to regard her feelings.

His best friend, Chuck Davis, dropped in a few days later. "I believe God's going to heal you."

Kurt looked at him. "I believe miracles happen. But let's face it. The odds are that I'm going to die. It might come with blinding speed. God does miracles for a purpose. I don't see any purpose here. Why doesn't anyone take my coming death as a serious possibility? Chuck, I'm ready to die. I don't have any sympathy for people who are afraid of death, especially for people who live in denial."

Chuck reached out and patted his friend on the shoulder. "You're right. I feel the same as you. I'm just thinking about

Meghan. You've got to allow her to have hope. She's struggling with this. It would be better for her if you didn't talk about death being inevitable or that you're ready for it."

"That's why you're my best friend. We don't have to hold back from one another. We can say anything that needs to be said. I'll be careful what I say around Meghan from now on. Thanks." Kurt hugged his best friend.

Another acquaintance saw Kurt and Meghan out walking a few days later. "Hello, Kurt. I've not seen you lately. When someone told me about your condition, I thought, *Kurt will improve. God's got lots of work for him to do in this world.* I hope you get well soon."

"Thank you." Kurt didn't say anything for a few minutes. He was busy thinking. *Everyone dies. I wonder if they had any idea as to what he would eventually die from if the cancer were healed.*

"No sermon about what Mr. Smith said?"

"What? Oh, no. I'm going to try to quit complaining. I know they mean well when they say things like that." He smiled at Meghan. She smiled back. The rest of the walk was quite pleasant.

What Next?

The chemotherapy treatments went on for around three months. The side effects were tolerable as far as Kurt was concerned. The diarrhea was no worse than before the chemo started. His hair became brittle and thinned a little. But unlike most patients, he didn't lose it. During the infusions, he sat and read. Over the three months, he read *War and Peace, Anna Karenina, Moby Dick, David Copperfield, The Idiot,* and *Crime and Punishment.* He was feeling better. Medications were taking care of the pain. After being so sick for six months, he now had a new and higher threshold of pain. Kurt thought, *If this is dying, it isn't that bad.* He was more relieved than he wanted anyone to know.

During the treatments, the clinic called him numerous times. A nutritionist, nurse navigator, financial navigator, and psychologist contacted him. Kurt accepted their advice and instructions. He was curious about seeing a psychologist though.

Why do I need to do that? Yet if everything the people at the cancer clinic recommended has been helpful thus far, I guess I'll go along with this too.

His first appointment with the psychologist was not until a few weeks after his last treatment. Dr. Talley's nurse welcomed him and went over his medical history. After that, Dr. Talley herself came to speak with him. She was a few years younger than Kurt. Her hair was short, blond, and curled. Kurt was surprised at her height. She was around five-eight and had green eyes and a strong chin. She didn't wear much makeup. Dr. Talley probably weighed around one hundred and fifty pounds. She was dressed in navy slacks with a plaid long-sleeved blouse. Much of the first session was just getting acquainted. They also went over some of his medications for depression and anxiety. The doctor decided to increase Kurt's dosage for one of the medications.

Dr. Talley looked at her notes. "I see that you have a PhD. What is it in?"

"History. I dropped out of college during my junior year but eventually returned and finished."

"That's interesting. It also says you were a branch manager at a bank for several years. When did you complete your education?"

"It was long after we were married and had kids. I started back to school after I was tired of banking." Anticipating her next question, he said, "I got married in 1980; we've been married nearly forty-five years. We have three children and six grandchildren."

"Wow! You've been married a long time. What are your goals

for therapy? In other words, what do you want to accomplish here?"

Kurt thought about it for a minute. "I don't have any goals. When the clinic contacted me, I made an appointment. I've followed the other advice the cancer clinic has offered, so I'm here."

"Some of your medications indicate problems with anxiety, depression, and sleep. Do you have problems with these issues?"

"I suppose so. I have trouble distinguishing between anxiety and depression. I guess I should just lay some of my problems out for you. I worry about my finances. I'm claustrophobic. At times I feel incredibly lonely, while other times I feel suffocated by the people around me. Most of the time, I'm frustrated by all the noise around me. I want peace and quiet. I love my wife, children, grandchildren, and pets, but our house is always too noisy. All I want is to be left alone and get some peace and quiet."

"You aren't anxious or depressed over the possibility that your illness is terminal?"

"No. I'm not afraid of dying. Dying is easy; it's living that is hard. I have my faith and am at peace with my Maker. I have friends and family. All you have to do to die is close your eyes and go to sleep. If you live, you have to wake up and face each day. That's what's hard."

Kurt looked around the room. He noticed some tiny bears holding honey pots.

"Those are cute."

"Thank you. You can put scented oil in the honey pot if you want to. I never do." She paused for a moment.

"Do you ever have thoughts of suicide?" She started writing some notes and shuffled a few papers. Kurt hadn't responded to her question. She looked at him with more intensity than previously.

"I've thought about suicide several times over the years. But don't worry, I'm not at risk to ever do it."

"Why not?"

He looked around the room. Then he closed his eyes. "I'm not sure. It's a combination of reasons." He opened his eyes and looked off into an imaginary distance. "First, my religious beliefs rule it out. Also, I suppose I'm something of a coward. I can't see myself doing anything that irrevocable; you can't take it back after doing it. After pondering it over the years, I've just ruled it out as a viable option."

"If you don't consider yourself at risk for suicide, and you aren't worried about death, how do you deal with the stress created by your depression and anxiety?"

The response was quick. "I eat. Whenever I feel a strong emotion, I binge eat until I can't find anything else to eat. It's more socially acceptable than drugs or alcohol in my circles. When something triggers me, I chow down."

Dr. Talley made an appointment to see Kurt again in two weeks. She asked him to call her Chrissie. She told Kurt it helped patients open up more than the more formal "Dr. Talley." She asked him to record the days and times he used stress eating until his next appointment and the reason for it, the trigger.

Kurt showed up for the next appointment, still not knowing what to expect. He did feel more comfortable with Dr. Talley after their initial session. After exchanging greetings, Kurt noted when and why he'd gone on several eating binges over the last two weeks. Dr. Talley discussed these with him for a few minutes. Kurt's anxiety was normal. His response to it was typical but not healthy.

"There is one thing that I find interesting in all of this. Many of your eating binges seem to center on clashes with your wife over the clutter in your office. Why does that cause so much trouble?"

"My wife likes things organized and neat. Anything that is out of place or messy upsets her. I tend to leave my office, especially my desk, with papers scattered all over it. That drives her crazy, but I'll probably never change."

"But it's your desk. If it's your office, why don't you tell her that's how you like it? That seems pretty reasonable."

"She considers everything in the house to be her territory. She decorates it. Cleans it. Decides what should be in it. And how it should look."

"But surely it's okay for you to have space just for you. Why can't you tell her that you prefer to have it that way instead of getting stressed-out and binge eating?"

Kurt just shrugged; he would never take Dr. Talley's suggestion. There was an uncomfortable pause in the conversation. Kurt didn't seem to know what to say.

They discussed some of the other causes of his eating binges. When the session was over, Dr. Talley gave Kurt some homework assignments. He was to continue tracking his eating binges and their causes. In addition, she wanted him to talk to his wife about his desk and explain that he needed some space that was his. Also, Kurt was supposed to discuss one or two other issues with his wife that tended to trigger eating binges. Dr. Talley felt he needed more time to do these things and suggested his next appointment be in three weeks rather than two. He agreed.

Kurt left the doctor's office, dreading doing his homework. These were not issues that he wanted to address. It would be easier to leave it alone. As he thought about it, Kurt knew he had gone along with many things he disliked to avoid conflict. Time was running out for him. Maybe the doctor's suggestions would make his last months or years better. He dreaded it, but he was going to try.

It took a few days for Kurt to get his courage up. One day, he felt ready to address it. "I'd like to talk to you about my desk. I know that you like it neat. You know that I like it cluttered. I try to help you keep the rest of the house neat. My office is in the back of the house. No one ever goes in there except me and the grandchildren. You go in to clean. But no one else ever goes in there. Would you please let me keep it my way, so I could have a small space that felt like it was mine?"

Meghan waited a few minutes before saying, "Okay, we'll try it."

Really! I can't believe it was this easy. He waited a while before he talked about anything else. One suggestion was to allow him to walk by himself occasionally—a walk without Meghan, without dogs—just some time to be alone with his thoughts. Meghan agreed again.

This was working well. Kurt would have never believed Meghan was letting him do these things. A week later, Kurt walked into his office. All the things he had on his desk had been placed in a basket on the corner of the desk. There was nothing else on the desk except for pictures and knickknacks. He asked Meghan about it.

"I agreed to try it. I gave it a week. I'm the one who cleans the house. You're no help. When we have company, they judge me by how the house looks. You keeping your desk a mess reflects badly on me. It makes me feel you don't care about me or respect me. I can't take it or put up with it."

I thought she agreed to it a little too readily. This is irritating. Particularly the remark about not being of any help. He dismissed it. The battle was over, and it ended the way he had expected it to end. But on the other hand, he could take walks by himself a few times a week. There was no blowback on that. It was at least one victory. She was sticking by that. He desperately needed that peace and quiet.

Three weeks later, he was back in Dr. Talley's office. She asked him about his homework. He went over his eating binges. Then he told her about the desk.

"At least now you know why she wants it that way. From her point of view, it's reasonable for her to want that."

Kurt almost argued back. It was as though she'd tricked him into asking for something she knew he wouldn't get. *I expected Chrissie to take my side and stick by me. She didn't. She was satisfied with Meghan's explanation. I guess it's a dead issue.*

He told her he was going for walks alone to get peace and quiet. She expressed happiness that Meghan had complied with that. Kurt had one defeat and one victory. The reasons for both conclusions were understandable.

"What were your feelings when you got your diagnosis from Dr. Ashraf?"

"It was what I expected. A little surreal."

"But what were you feeling? Were you angry? Were you sad? Were you shocked? What ran through your mind immediately after hearing your diagnosis? Be specific."

Kurt thought for a few minutes. "I felt a sense of relief. I was a little bit scared. But mainly, I thought, *it's almost over*. It was a peaceful feeling."

"Why? Why would you feel relief? Why was it a peaceful feeling? The scared is easy to understand. What was the other thing—yes, you said you thought, 'it's almost over.' That's a curious thing to say."

"Well, there was relief in finally getting a correct diagnosis. I was tired of running to different doctors and hospitals and feeling like they were wasting my time. I felt like Dr. Ashraf was spot-on."

Chrissie got up. She walked across the room and picked up another folder. She looked at it for a minute. Then she carried it back to her seat. Kurt patiently waited. He fiddled with his cane while she did all of this. *I wonder what she's up to. Everything she does has a purpose. I guess I'll find out soon enough.*

"Is that everything? I don't think it is. Why did you say those other things?"

"I suppose the peaceful feeling and the idea that 'it's almost over' come from other things in my life. I'm sort of tired of living. I'm ready for life to be over. I've lived a long time and played by all the rules. I've tried my best to do what is right. And I've been miserable. I'm tired of having to go off alone to weep. I'm tired of smiling and laughing when what I want to do is cry. I'm tired of following rules that have made me bitter and unhappy. I'm ready to close my eyes, fall asleep, and not wake up. Every day, I wake up. I spend the day saying and doing things I don't want to say or do. I spend my days with people I don't want to be with. I'm tired of it all. I'm ready to call it a day and get some rest."

Dr. Talley had been busy taking notes earlier. Now she laid her pen down. She looked at Kurt with new interest. He was a puzzle, and she was trying to put the pieces together, but something didn't fit.

"That's quite a statement. Do you mean all of that? Or are you having a pity party? Why do you have to pretend? Who is it you do or don't want to be with?

I'm having a hard time following your answers. On the surface, most people would be jealous of your life and fight like crazy to hang on to it. You don't seem to care. Either you're not telling the truth, or you're leaving some critical information out. Which is it?"

Kurt frowned. His gaze was fixed on something far away. It was apparent he didn't want to answer her question. Dr. Talley remained silent. This annoyed Kurt. He hoped she would drop this line and move on to something else. After what seemed like an eternity, he looked down at the floor.

"I'm sure that I'm exaggerating. Also, I'm leaving a lot of information out."

There! I answered her. Now she'll drop it. He raised his eyes and saw she was still staring at him. *She's like a dog that's got hold of a bone. Nothing I do or say will make her let go of this. I guess I knew it would eventually come to this. I give up.* Once again, Kurt looked up, but not at Dr. Talley. He looked into the distance, even though they were in a small room.

"The truth is that I'm skipping the real story of my life. You're only getting the pretend story of my life."

"Okay, that is pretty interesting. We've got to look into that, but there are some other things I want to ask you first."

Then she began speaking and took the conversation in a new direction. She caught Kurt off guard.

"You've had a very long and successful career in two fields. You are well-educated. You have a long, stable marriage, children, and grandchildren.

There was no record of serious health issues in your life until the cancer occurred. You are persuasive when you say you are not afraid of death or dying. Why are you depressed? Your life seems to be the American dream realized. What is it that is bothering you? Why are you unable to enjoy all that you've accomplished? These are the things we need to discuss."

Kurt sat there for a few moments, staring off into space. He couldn't respond. It seemed that there was no way to answer.

After another long, awkward silence, he replied, "I don't know. I am sometimes happy and thankful for all the blessings in my life. Still, I have this overwhelming sense of failure and frustration. I'm not a happy person. I act happy and put a good face on it in public, but I'm a basket case when I'm alone."

"How long have you felt this way?"

"For nearly fifty years," came the quick reply.

"So this began before you were married?"

"Yes. I suppose it began at least four years before that," Kurt answered slowly.

"Then you must know what this is all about. Tell me about it. Why were you so afraid to ask your wife about your desk?"

More silence followed. Kurt still had a faraway, distant

expression. Suddenly, he looked at Chrissie as though he had made a decision and began to talk.

"I never argue about the office or the desk because I feel guilty."

"Why do you feel guilty?" She had laid her notes and pen down again. Her eyes were focused on Kurt and nothing else. She was hanging on every word. It was a combination of surprise and deep interest. She was absorbed in the things he was saying. It was as though she couldn't wait to hear what he would say next.

"Because I wasn't in love with Meghan when I married her. I feel I'm responsible for a lot of the unhappiness in her life. Trying to keep my office a little more like she likes isn't unreasonable for someone I've injured like I've injured her."

"If you weren't in love with her, why did you get married?"

"Because I was depressed. Suicidal. She was the first date I'd had in years that could make me laugh. Meghan is a nice person. She was a good friend who helped me through a hard time. She saved my life. I do love her, but not with a burning, passionate love."

"There are a lot of different types of love. Did you ever have, as you describe it, 'burning, passionate love' with anyone?"

Kurt waited a few moments. "Yes. I did. But things didn't work out. I don't talk about it with anyone but my best friend."

"I think we've found what we need to talk about. Let's pick it up here at your next session. It would be good for you to tell someone else about this thing that has depressed you for half a century."

"Your homework for our next session is to start with whatever happened fifty years ago to make you feel all these things. Think about it. Organize your thoughts and tell me about them, and I'll see you in two weeks."

"I won't need to organize them or think about them. They

are so burned in my memory that I could tell you anytime. There isn't any need for preparation."

With that, Kurt left. Over the subsequent sessions, Kurt told his story to someone other than his best friend for the first time. It was difficult at first. But the more he talked about it, the more it helped give him a sense of release—a trickle of words developed into a torrent. The story of Kurt Kellerman's life was laid bare.

Chapter 2
The Story Begins

Acquaintances

Kurt Kellerman first noticed Mary Johnson during junior high band. He was a year older and knew little about her other than that she was pretty, played the French horn, and had a boyfriend. That was the extent of their relationship for the next few years.

Mary moved to town when she was ten with her sister Lori, her brother Sam, her baby brother Joey, and their mother. They didn't seem to have much money. Mary was fun, pretty, and intelligent. She loved music and dancing. Her family was Roman Catholic. She developed many friends and acquaintances and was well-liked by everyone.

On the other hand, Kurt was a lifelong resident of the community. He was the youngest of three children. His older siblings were popular. He wasn't as outgoing as them but was a good student. They had a decent house and a decent car and never went hungry. Kurt made excellent grades but was a mediocre athlete. His parents were well respected in the community. They didn't have much money, but most people in the community didn't. Kurt's father owned a hardware store. He was also a strong fundamentalist Christian who condemned drinking, dancing, gambling, and several other social activities. Kurt was terrified when it came to dancing and girls. He was too shy to have a girlfriend, but he decided to take the plunge toward the end of his freshman year of high school.

He began with baby steps. Kurt overcame his shyness and began to talk to girls he found attractive. Earlier in life, if a girl spoke to him, he disappeared. Now, as awkward and nervous as he was, he tried to converse with them. Some were disasters. Kurt wasn't good at small talk. He didn't know how to flirt. But he was making progress.

There were girls whom he had crushes on in elementary school and junior high, but he assumed they never knew of his interest. He was terrified of them. Some boy-girl parties in seventh and eighth grade helped him a little, but this would be a long journey. Mary was at some of these parties, and he sometimes spoke to her because his crushes were on girls his age. They became acquaintances.

Kurt was around four-ten and one hundred pounds. He wore glasses, had straight golden hair with bangs that brushed his eyebrows, and bright blue eyes with long lashes. He had a slightly pug nose and a mischievous grin. Kurt was never sure how much he appealed to females. He had always been so awkward and uncomfortable that he was filled with anxiety and self-doubt. His friend Rudy always told him he looked like a member of the Hitler Youth, the perfect German. Kurt wasn't sure if this was a compliment or an insult. It just made him even less secure.

Summers in small-town USA in the 1970s meant two things to teens under sixteen: the public swimming pool and the local baseball/softball fields. You hung out at the pool in the afternoon and the ballfield in the evening. You could ride your bike there and see a lot of kids. Kurt became more experienced in talking with girls in a group or occasionally alone.

Mary didn't go to the ballfields often but was at the pool almost daily. She always brought her preschool brother Joey with her. She was responsible for taking care of him. This made Mary stand out a little to Kurt. *She's responsible. She's pretty too.* Mary had medium-brown eyes, brown hair down to her shoulders that perfectly matched her eyes, a dark complexion, pretty teeth, and a sweet smile. Mary was five foot three and weighed about one hundred and five pounds. She had a lovely figure; guys would stop and stare when she walked by. Mary was also very popular. It seemed like every boy in town wanted to go out with her.

Toward the end of his freshman year in high school, Kurt had a girlfriend. They hung out together all the time. Debra Mueller had long, straight golden hair that fell gracefully over her shoulders. She had light blue eyes that twinkled and fair skin with just a few freckles. She was five foot five and weighed about one hundred twenty-five pounds. Kurt took Debra to the local pizza place, Gino's. They went to some parties where Spin the Bottle was played. He took her to a local ice cream shop for a treat. Kurt was having a good time. Without warning, Debra started dating a fellow a few years older (with a driver's license), Rick Jamerson. He was able to take her to movies and concerts and bought her a lot of gifts. It was very different for her than going out with Kurt.

It hurt a little, but Kurt moved on. His next girlfriend was Karen Smith. This was at the beginning of his sophomore year. They were just good friends more than boyfriend and girlfriend. He took her to the homecoming dance. They broke up on the Monday after and were still good friends. It was no big deal.

Kurt's next girlfriend was Jenny Rideout. She was a year younger but much more active in dating than anyone Kurt had known before. Her family had money and were unhappy that she was interested in Kurt. When her father found out that Jenny was going out with Kurt, he called her into the living room and had her sit down.

"What are you doing, hanging out with that Kellerman boy? There are lots of other boys in town, from the right kind of families, that would love to take you out."

"Kurt is a nice boy. His father owns a hardware store, and they even live in our neighborhood. I don't understand what the big deal is." Jenny could be defiant.

Her mother joined in the argument at that point. "You will not talk back to your father! You can do a lot better than the Kellermans. Listen to your father!"

Jenny was angry by now. Her face was red. "You can't tell me who I can and can't date! I'll see anyone I want."

"The next time I catch you with Kurt Kellerman, you'll be grounded for a week. I know that Rick Evans would like to go out with you. Why don't you think about him? He's nice-looking, and his father has an excellent job. They live in the nicest neighborhood in town." Mr. Rideout was eyeing Jenny for any signs of defiance. He stood over her. Jenny decided it was best to remain quiet.

Jenny saw Kurt at school the next day. "My parents threatened to ground me if I didn't stop seeing you. I told them I could see whoever I wanted. Would you like to get together after school today?"

"Sure. I'll meet you as soon as the bell rings."

They walked in a park in the middle of town, held hands, laughed, and talked. From out of nowhere, Mr. Rideout pulled up beside them in his car.

"Young lady, you get in this car right now! You're grounded for a week. And you, boy, stay away from my daughter if you know what's good for you."

Jenny got into her father's car. Kurt watched them drive off. The next day, they met again after school. It felt very romantic and melodramatic. Both of them vowed to let nothing stop them from seeing one another. Her parents had arranged a date for Jenny with Rick Evans on the evening her grounding was over.

She continued to date Rick to please her parents but also kept secret rendezvous with Kurt. They sneaked around for months, never seeing one another in public. If her parents had not made their ban, Kurt and Jenny would probably have broken up after a few weeks. Instead, they saw one another for at least six months before they parted.

Kurt went out with a few other girls over time but was not interested in anyone. There were numerous girls he was attracted to, but no one special. He now had his driver's license. He drove a 1970 Ford with a very weak engine but a nice sky-blue paint job. Most of the time, he ran around with his buddies and acted foolishly like a sixteen-year-old boy. He didn't drink. He didn't do drugs. He went to church with his parents. Sometimes it offended him that when the police did sobriety checks, they just waved him on through because they knew searching his car would be a waste of everyone's time. But life was moving along.

Friends

During the period after breaking up with Jenny Rideout, Kurt seemed to bump into Mary a little more often. They spent more time together at band activities. He noticed she and her brother Joey had made a Yogi Bear snowman in front of their house during a big snow. A few days later, he talked to Mary about it.

"How on earth did you sculpt it?"

"It was easy. We just got a huge mound of snow and some small shovels and also used our hands to smooth it out until it looked like Yogi Bear."

"I'm jealous. I could never have done that and got it right."

"By the way, I'm having a party for my sixteenth birthday in late January. You're invited if you would like to come."

"Thank you. I'd love to. Let me know the exact time and date. I'll be there."

This caused Kurt to start thinking. One of his buddies, Tommy English, was going out with Mary. She was inviting him as a friend. But during their silly little discussion of a snowman, Kurt realized he was interested in being more than just an acquaintance or friend of Mary. He debated back and forth on going to the party. Finally, he decided to go but only stayed a short time. Seeing Mary having a great time with Tommy bothered him, so after around thirty minutes, Kurt said his goodbyes and left.

They continued to bump into one another. Sometimes they would sit together at a high school basketball game. One day, Tommy and Kurt were hanging out after school.

"I broke up with Mary yesterday. I decided I wanted to go out with Emily Snicker."

Kurt was amazed. "Why did you break up with Mary? I thought you liked her. The two of you were always together."

Tommy shrugged. "The whole thing had got old. I was just ready for something different. Emily is nice, and she's got a great figure. I've got a date with her Saturday night."

Tommy is nuts, breaking up with Mary. Does this mean I should ask her out? Yes. He was going to ask Mary out. As popular as she was, he'd better move quickly. He tried for a couple of days to get the nerve up. On Thursday, he finally had enough courage. He had band with Mary during first period. He would try to talk to her at the end of first period and maybe walk her to her second class. All through band practice, he was shaking. He made numerous mistakes. Kurt was in the trumpet section. He planned to put his trumpet away, cut over to the door, and meet Mary as she left. She played the French horn. Their cases were much farther from the door, so it took her a little more time to get things put away and out the door than anyone from the trumpets.

About halfway through class, Rudy Ackerman, who sat beside Kurt, whispered to him, "Have you heard the latest?"

Kurt just looked at Rudy. They had been close friends for the last six years. Rudy was much more worldly than Kurt. Their differences seemed to be the source of their friendship. Rudy took the blank expression on Kurt's face for a no.

"See Mary Johnson over there? She and Tommy English broke up, and now she's going out with Keith Mueller."

Kurt just said, "Oh. No, I hadn't heard that. I'm surprised she's going out with Mueller. Of course, she could go out with almost anyone she wanted."

"She sure could. I was going to try to take her out, but Mueller must have got the jump on her. It doesn't matter. I didn't have a chance, but I figured it was worth a try."

That ended the conversation. It looked like he and Rudy would be hanging out together over the weekend. That was a big disappointment.

Kurt and Mary still bumped into one another and talked now and then, but much less than before. She and Keith Mueller were together all the time. Kurt didn't know anyone he wanted to date, so he spent most of his time running around with his friends. He still had the occasional date, but they were double dates to hang out with one of his buddies.

They continued as friends for the remainder of the school year. They saw one another at the public swimming pool in the summer. Sometimes they ran into one another by chance somewhere else. Mary was still dating Keith.

One evening, Kurt was at home and started looking through his high school yearbook from his junior year. He read the autographed notes from his friends. The words in one of the messages jumped off the page at him. He hadn't noticed it before. Most of the notes were just silly jokes or best wishes and such. This was a little more than the usual stuff, at least in Kurt's mind.

"To a very good-looking and sweet guy whom in the past year I've grown very fond of." More typical comments followed this. It was from Mary. He sat up and reread the lines several times. That night, he decided if the opportunity presented itself, he wouldn't waste time getting up the nerve to ask Mary for a date.

Just after July 4, word went around that Mary and Keith were no longer dating. The small-town ritual of teenagers cruising all through the evening was in full force in their little town. People drove laps around Ron's Twirly Top (a drive-in that served mainly burgers, sodas, and ice cream), the public square, and the public swimming pool. A full lap was nearly three miles and took about eight to ten minutes, depending on how long it took to get around Ron's. It was a way to see who was out and about, what was going on, and possibly find someone to hang out with.

It just happened that Kurt and his friend "Racket" Farris were cruising together on a Saturday. Racket had picked up his nickname for his love of tennis. He spent most of his time every summer driving or playing tennis. As they circled through Ron's, they saw Mary and a friend. Kurt suggested Racket pull in and park by Mary. "Hello. What are the two of you up to tonight?"

"We don't have anything going on. I don't have to babysit Joey tonight, so I called Pam and thought we'd both get out of the house for a while."

"Would you like to get in with us for a while? We're just out looking for something to do."

"That would be great. Let me find somewhere to leave my car. Just follow us. I don't think the bank's parking lot is full tonight."

When they got to the bank, both cars pulled in and parked.

Mary and her friend Pam got into Racket's car, and the four continued cruising and talking.

Racket was determined to play a practical joke on his friend Pete. Kurt was not thrilled with Racket's brainstorm but was glad to be in the car with Mary, so he didn't speak up. The plan was to find something disgusting and put it in the driver's seat of Pete's car. Kurt went along but was terrified this would turn Mary off, as she was a very nice girl.

Racket was still trying to come up with ideas when Pam saw a dead cat on the side of the road. The two of them got out, picked it up, and then took it to Pete's car, which was parked at a grocery store that was closed along the cruise route. They put the cat in Pete's car and returned to Racket's car, laughing like hyenas.

When Racket and Pam got out to play the joke, Kurt got into the back seat with Mary. But the joke wasn't funny.

Good grief! Racket has ruined everything. I'm here with Mary. I'm sitting beside her. But Racket and Pam are talking about putting a dead cat in someone's car. I'm doomed.

He tried to think of something to discuss, but Racket and Pam kept returning to the dead cat. Mary was quiet, and Kurt assumed she was disgusted with the whole thing. He'd started the night so hopefully, but things had taken a very wrong turn. *Will Mary ever go out with me after this? Everything was going so well, and now, a fiasco. I'm going to kill Racket.* They cruised for another hour and then returned to the bank parking lot. The girls got in their car and left.

Chapter 3
August 1974

Taking a Chance

Kurt didn't get out much for a few days. He worked at his father's hardware store that summer and was glad to be distracted by it. Every day he worked from 7:00 a.m. until 5:00 p.m. The only day he took off that summer was to take the ACT, which most of the colleges in the area accepted. The SAT wasn't offered. It would take an hour to drive to the test, plus an hour to return, so Kurt didn't worry about taking the SAT.

What bothered him was whether he would work at the store during the school year. He didn't mind working, but he'd played football for three years and wanted to go out again his senior year. Finally, Kurt got up the nerve to talk to his father about it. He was worried he was letting him down, but the answer surprised him.

Mr. Kellerman looked like an older version of Kurt. His hair was dark brown instead of the golden brown of Kurt's, but they had the same blue eyes, pug nose, and jaw lines. His father was five feet eight inches tall, weighed about one hundred ninety pounds, and wore glasses. They often used the same hand gestures and mannerisms.

Kurt yawned, something he did when he was nervous. "Dad, I know you are counting on me to help at the store this year, but I'd like to play one more football season. I don't want to leave you in a bind, so tell me what you think."

"Son, you've got the rest of your life to work. There's nothing wrong with wanting to play your final season of football. I love watching you play and wouldn't want you to miss it. I've already got someone in mind to help at the store, so just let me know when practices start so I can have you help train him."

Wow! That went well. Maybe I should run by Mary's house and talk to her.

Maybe Racket's crazy antics have ruined things, but I'll never know unless I try.

Two-a-day practices started on Monday, August 19, with equipment pickup on Friday, August 16. Mr. Kellerman told Kurt he could stop working on Thursday, August 15.

Kurt decided to get cleaned up after work, drop by Mary's house, and see what happened. When he pulled up, Mary was outside watching her six-year-old brother, Joey, playing in the yard. She smiled and waved when she saw Kurt. He got out of the car. "Hello."

She got up from a lawn chair to greet him as he walked toward her. "Hello, I thought you'd disappeared for the past week or two. I enjoyed cruising with you the other night."

Relief flooded through Kurt's mind and body. "About that, I wanted to apologize for Racket's practical joke. I was pretty uncomfortable with it and thought maybe you were too. If it did bother you, I'm sorry."

She smiled again. "I knew it wasn't your idea. If you were truly the person I think you are, you would drop by and apologize for it. You're one of the nicest boys in town. I'm glad to know that I was right about that. Joey! Let's take a walk around the block."

Kurt walked with Mary and Joey as they strolled. It took Kurt a minute to say, "I'm so relieved to hear you say that. I was so embarrassed I couldn't face you for ten days. You didn't seem to be the sort of girl who would like that sort of thing. It was gross."

"How did Pete take it?"

"Pete laughed his head off. He figured it was Racket but asked me first. I assume he's got something special he's planning in return now. He's as crazy as Racket. I guess that's why they're friends. What did Pam think of it?"

"She's as crazy as they are. She thought it was a great night." Mary laughed. "Will you work at the hardware store during the school year?"

"No. I talked it over with Dad, and he said I should enjoy playing football for one last year. He told me I had the rest of my life to work. He's already got one of the Bowling boys lined up to work the school year."

"He sounds like a nice man."

"He is. I was wondering if you are busy with anything this weekend?"

Mary's smile went away. "I'm sorry. But yes, I have some family things going on Friday and Saturday."

"That's all right. I hope you have a nice time."

The rest of the walk was spent making sure that Joey didn't get into trouble. He wanted to jump down into a creek. He claimed Mary was mean and appealed to Kurt for help. Kurt sided with Mary. Joey said he was ready to go home, so they went home. When they returned, Mrs. Johnson called out that it was time to come in and help with dinner. Kurt and Mary said goodbye to one another, and he left.

Mary was now a grown woman. She was five-six and weighed one hundred twenty pounds. She still had the same penetrating brown eyes, tanned skin, and brown hair that fell on her shoulders. Mary had a great figure and the sweetest smile he'd ever seen. She was beautiful. Kurt could lose himself in looking at her.

The following week, Kurt was busy with work until Thursday evening. He picked up his football equipment at the fieldhouse on Friday morning. He measured 5'11" and weighed 150 pounds. After caring for a few other things Friday afternoon, he visited Mary. He pulled up, and again, she was in the yard with Joey.

"I'm sorry about last weekend. I didn't know if you'd ever be back." Mary smiled.

That smile was so arresting that it was hard for Kurt to think or say anything. Finally, he blurted, "I've just been busy at the store and getting ready for football season. I hope you had a good time."

Kurt saw Joey run into the house. *Is something wrong?*

Mary noticed it too. "He's probably just getting another toy." A minute later, Joey came running out with something in his hands. Then Joey chucked whatever it was on Kurt's car. Kurt's eyes widened. Joey had thrown two eggs on his car.

Mary asked, "Why did you do that, Joey?"

"When he's here, you don't play with me!"

"Go to your room, Joey!"

With an angry look, he walked back into the house.

"I've not been here very often. Does he dislike me?"

"He wants me all to himself. Let me get some rags and a bucket of soapy water. We need to wash that off your car."

That was the most fun Kurt had ever had washing a car. He thought of Mary almost every time he washed a car for the rest of his life. Somehow she made everything more fun. They laughed quite a bit about the whole incident. After finishing, Kurt asked, "Do you think Joey would like it if we took him for a ride?"

"I'll go get him. He'll love it."

Kurt got in, and Joey slid in next to him with Mary on the other side of the front seat. They cruised around town for a while. Kurt went by the drive-thru window at the local Dairy Queen and got everyone a Coke. Joey got an ice cream cone too. After about thirty minutes, they went back to Mary's house.

She said, "I think he likes you now."

Kurt laughed. "I don't know anything about little boys or little girls. Bribery is my only tool."

Mary giggled. They started talking about the coming school year. She also explained she'd had to babysit for Joey and her niece the previous weekend. Between the two of them, she was swamped. As they talked, a car pulled into the driveway. Kurt recognized one of the people as Lori, Mary's older sister, but not the two men who got out. Mary said hello to them as they went into the house. Then she continued talking with Kurt. After about five minutes, Lori shouted out the front door that Mary needed to come into the house.

Kurt said, "Am I interrupting something? If I am, I apologize."

Mary frowned. "No! You're not interrupting anything. That's my sister and her husband. She's brought someone here to meet me. She thinks she should play matchmaker or something. I don't want to meet him, and I don't want to go in there." Lori called out a second time.

"How about this? Why don't you go on in and keep your sister happy? But I would like to ask you out for next Saturday night. We'll see *The Sting* at the Star-View Drive-In if that's all right. If you don't want to, I understand."

Mary again smiled that wonderful smile. "I'd love to. I can't wait."

"I'll pick you up at 7:00 next Saturday night. I'll get in touch with you again before then." He drove away feeling happier than he had all summer.

It was a busy week for Kurt. Football practice at 6:00 every morning meant setting his alarm for 5:00, which was tough for someone who was not a morning person. Still, it was only around eighty degrees at that time of day. By the time practice was over at 8:30, the temperature had rocketed to ninety. The humidity was so thick that people broke into a sweat just standing still. After two and a half hours of practice, his energy was exhausted.

After practice, Kurt went home and cooled off. Then he rested. After a light lunch, Kurt went to the swimming pool on Monday afternoon. Sure enough, Mary was there with Joey. After saying hello and talking about each one's day, Kurt asked, "How did things go last weekend with Lori and her friend?"

Mary laughed. "He didn't seem to enjoy my company very much. He wanted to know who you were. I told him you were the person I was dating. Lori went ballistic. It was a very awkward visit." She smiled as she told him about her sister's attempt at setting her up with someone.

Kurt said, "I'm sorry if I caused trouble between you and your sister. I should admit that I'm not sorry that I may have interfered with her matchmaking."

"Lori is always blowing up about something. It was funny that Terry, her husband, took my side. He told her she was mental for trying to fix me up. Even Mom said Lori needed to quit trying to run my life. I feel slightly bad for the guy they brought from Paducah, but I didn't even know they were bringing him until two hours before they arrived. I told Lori not to bring him, but she insisted. It's all worked out, so let's discuss something else."

They discussed football practice and Saturday night. Kurt didn't really know much about Mary's family life and asked about her parents and why she was always taking care of Joey. For once, he saw Mary look truly sad. He noticed her eyes were a medium brown that seemed to convey as much as her words.

Those eyes penetrated in a way he'd never been aware that eyes could. They noticed everything, yet they seemed to speak too. They were the most beautiful eyes he'd ever seen or ever would.

"My father was a farmer. We lived about thirty miles from here. Dad was the most wonderful man in the world. I was his little princess. When I was ten, he was killed in a farming accident. I was heartbroken. We moved here because we have some relatives around. It was my mom, my brother Sam, Lori, Joey, and me. Joey was just a baby when all of this happened. Mom's health was never very good. It became my job to take care of him. Lori did some of it but married when she graduated from high school last year. She and Terry live in Paducah. Sam got married and moved thirty minutes from here. So now it's all up to me."

This was new information for Kurt. *Mary has the responsibilities of an adult. If I could help her, I would. She's incredible. I want to make her happy. She's had too much sorrow in her life.*

After a few hours at the pool, Kurt went home. He went to football practice and came home exhausted again. Going to the pool had been a mistake. On Tuesday and Wednesday, he rested between practices. On Thursday, he went to the pool again. Mary wasn't there, so he drove by her house. They visited for a few hours. School started the following Monday, and the only football practice would be after school until around 6:00 each night. Games were on Friday nights at 7:00 or 8:00, starting the Friday after Labor Day.

Saturday finally rolled around. Kurt was nervous all day. He washed and cleaned his car. He decided to get a haircut at Smith's barber shop. Then he tried to figure out what to wear and what music to play in the car. He settled on some khaki pants and a light blue shirt. Simon and Garfunkel's Greatest Hits seemed like a good choice. It had a mix of romantic and rock music that wouldn't send the wrong message.

As the day passed, he decided to show up no earlier than

6:55 p.m. and no later than 7:00. He wanted to be a few minutes early or right on time but not super early or even one second late. The car was gassed up, and he took off. He drove within a block of Mary's house and saw that it was ten minutes till the hour. The decision was made to circle Ron's Drive-In once and then pick up Mary. He parked at 6:56 p.m. and went straight to the door. Mary opened the door almost immediately after he knocked. She had on a red blouse and white slacks. Her brown hair fell just past her shoulders.

"Come in." Kurt entered the house and sat down.

"Goodbye, Mom."

"What's the name of the boy you're going with tonight?"

"It's Kurt Kellerman. He's a very nice boy. Joey, be a good boy for Mom. Bye-bye."

They walked out the door. He opened the door of his sky-blue Ford, and she slid across the bench seat. He got in on the driver's side and started the car. They drove a few laps around town before heading for the movie. It wouldn't start playing until 8:00 or 8:30. As they made their way around Ron's Drive-In, several people stopped whatever they were doing and stared.

Kurt could read their minds. "Kellerman on a date with Johnson? He's way out of his league and out of his mind." He didn't care. Kurt was happy. Mary seemed happy too.

As they drove, Kurt commented, "The gossip chain will be busy all weekend. Did you see the looks on their faces?"

"Yes, I did. They couldn't believe I was going out with someone as nice and popular as you."

Kurt gave her a surprised look. *How on earth did Mary ever get it in her head that I'm popular?* "No. It's sweet of you to say that, but I'm not popular. They couldn't believe I was going out with the prettiest and sweetest girl in the school."

They both broke out laughing. Mary slipped her hand in his as they drove down the highway. The movie was entertaining but the least important thing on either person's mind. Kurt put his arm around her, and they nestled together happily.

On the way home from the movie, Kurt said, "I have a couple of questions for you. First, I should have asked, but what time do I need to get you home? Second, why did you go out with me?"

"I should be home by 11:00 p.m., so we're fine. Even 11:30 would be all right, but it depends on Mom's mood. As for the other question, I wanted to go out with you because you're nice. You're the first boy that's ever asked about my father. Who asked why I'm always babysitting Joey. A few guys noticed I was always babysitting him, but they complained. You asked because you cared. That's what I want in a relationship. Why did you want to go out with me?"

Although Kurt should have seen this question coming, it surprised him. "Are you kidding? You're the prettiest girl in school. I love your smile. You're kind. You're honest. You're smart. I don't know why anyone wouldn't want to take you out. I can't believe you said yes to me."

They both laughed a little more. Kurt pulled up in front of Mary's house five minutes before eleven. He got out and then opened her door to help her out. They walked to the door. At the top of the steps, she turned and reached up; he bent, and they kissed. It felt like an intoxicating drug. Kurt would have liked to stay there for hours, but they pulled apart. They said good night to each other, and Mary went into the house.

Kurt must have walked back to his car, but he didn't know, or care, how he got there. He drove straight home. Lots of guys got together after dropping their dates off and hung out for a while. Kurt wasn't interested. His evening had ended on a high note. His first kiss with Mary. Anything after that could only be a disappointment; when he arrived home, he got ready for bed and went to his room. He lay looking out his bedroom window at the stars, trying to remember everything that went on during the date. He was too excited to sleep but dozed off. It was the perfect end to a fantastic day.

Kurt got up and went to church with his parents the following day. He couldn't wait to get home. After a large Sunday dinner, he called Mary. Her family's phone was unlisted, but she'd given him the number last night. Kurt hoped he could come over during the afternoon.

Mary answered the phone. "Hello?"

"Hello. This is Kurt. I wondered if you were busy this afternoon."

"Yes, I am. I'm sorry, it's a family thing. Last night was great, and I'm looking forward to seeing you at school tomorrow."

"Thank you. I'm looking forward to seeing you too. Have a nice day."

"You too. Goodbye." Mary hung up.

Kurt was disappointed. That afternoon, he found a few other things to do. He was looking forward to school for the first time in his life.

The first day of school was only for half of the day. Students knew their homerooms but not their class schedules. They received the schedules during homeroom on the first day. Kurt discovered he had band with Mary during first period, chemistry during fourth, and study hall during seventh. He'd never had any classes with her in previous years other than band. *This is great! I don't know how this happened, but everything is going my way.* The students received their books and had brief introductions to each class, and school dismissed a little before noon.

Kurt walked Mary to her car in the parking lot and then got in his car to go home. On the way home, Kurt noticed Jenny Rideout following him. He pulled in at his house, and Mary pulled in behind him from out of nowhere. Jenny drove on by with an angry look on her face. Kurt asked, "What was that all about?"

"She decided since we'd gone out that maybe she was more

interested in you than she thought. I overheard her talking in the girls' gym this morning. I just thought I'd send her a little message."

Kurt laughed. "You didn't need to. That relationship is dead and gone. But I'm glad you dropped by."

"What are you doing the rest of the day?"

"I have football practice at 3:30, but I don't have anything going on until then. Would you like to spend a few hours together this afternoon?"

"I'll be babysitting Joey this afternoon, but you're welcome to come over."

"If it's all right with your mother, I'll be over in about fifteen to twenty minutes."

"See you then. Joey can be a handful." With that, Mary drove off.

Kurt went into the house and grabbed a sandwich and his practice uniform. His mother was folding some laundry. "What are you doing this afternoon?"

"I'm going to help Mary babysit her little brother. Then I'm going to football practice."

She walked into the kitchen. "What time will you be home tonight? And who is Mary?"

"By the time practice is over and I shower, it will be a few minutes after 6:00. Mary Johnson is her name. I went out with her on Saturday. She's a junior this year. You've seen her. She plays French horn in band."

Mrs. Kellerman was forty-seven. She was a 5'4" brunette and weighed one hundred fifty pounds. Her eyes were gray-blue. Her nose was a little long and slightly crooked from having broken it as a little girl.

Kurt headed out the door. Mary and Joey were still eating lunch when he arrived. Mary's mother ate in her room. She called out to Mary and wanted to know who'd come to the door. Mary told her it was Kurt and went back to her mother's room.

She came back carrying her mother's dirty dishes and put them in the sink.

"Is it okay for me to be here? Is your mother sick?"

"I promise it's fine for you to be here. Mom isn't sick. She has a lot of back problems and stays in bed most of the time when I'm home. She gets around and takes care of Joey when I'm gone." After lunch, Mary washed and Kurt dried the dishes.

Joey went into his room to play, so the couple sat on the sofa and talked. There was nothing important to say that day. It was all about the foolish things teenagers liked to talk about: music, movies, school gossip, and such.

Later, they took Joey outside. He liked to play with cars and trucks in a little dirt pile. Joey spent the rest of the afternoon building roads and bridges for his cars and trucks. In no time at all, it was time for Kurt to leave for practice.

Before going, Kurt asked Mary if they could go out on Saturday. Mary said yes. Kurt promised to call after practice and discuss what they would do on Saturday night. Then he drove straight to practice. After three hours, he came home, ate dinner, and called Mary.

Meet the Family

When Mary answered the phone, she asked about football practice. They talked about what they thought their classes would be like. Kurt expressed his pleasant surprise that they had three classes together. Finally, Kurt brought up his plans for Saturday evening. He hoped they could spend the afternoon together as well. There was an awkward pause on the other end of the line.

Mary said, "We need to change our plans."

"Why? What's wrong?" He sounded anxious.

"It's just that most of my family is coming in for Labor Day weekend. Mom says I need to spend Friday and Saturday with them. I think they're all leaving on Sunday. But she said I could invite you to come while they're here. If you want to."

Kurt listened with apprehension. *What kind of change? She sure spends a lot of time on family events. Oh! She wants me to come.*

"That would be great! I thought you were getting ready to tell me something awful. I can't get to your house on Friday until 6:00 or 6:30. Will that work for you and your family?" You could hear the relief in his voice.

"That will be fine. I need to warn you that it will be a big group. My sister Lori and her husband Terry Norris, my brother Sam, his wife Nancy, their baby Little Sammy, and my brother Bob and his three-year-old daughter Lisa. Then there's Mom, Joey, and me. Does that scare you off?

Kurt laughed. "I'm used to big families. I have more than thirty first cousins. I'm just glad to be with you. Just let me know when I need to be there."

The rest of the week consisted of attending school, football practice, and calling Mary after getting home. The plan for Friday was to go out for pizza and roller-skating as soon as Kurt arrived. This made Kurt nervous. He was not a very good skater. The last time he'd tried, it was all he could do to stay on his feet. The time before that, he'd fallen and chipped a tooth. Kurt wanted to make a good impression on Mary's family, but this had disaster written all over it. He warned Mary he wasn't very good but assured her he was looking forward to Friday night.

After hearing the plans for Friday night, Kurt was puzzled. When his married brother and sister came home, it was boring. They didn't go out for pizza. They certainly didn't go roller-skating. Everyone sat around talking. His brother and brother-in-law tried to impress one another with their income, finances, and social standing. His sister and sister-in-law debated politics. His sister was a radical left Democrat (George McGovern had been too conservative for her), and his sister-in-law was a country club Republican (a huge Nelson Rockefeller fan). It was the definition of boring. This family get-together was going to be very different.

Finally, Friday came. Kurt told Mary goodbye after school and hurried to practice. Mary's family wanted to head out for pizza as soon as possible. When practice was over and he'd showered, Kurt sped home. He changed clothes and headed over to Mary's. There were three additional cars parked in front of the house. Everyone was there. Kurt parked and knocked on the door. It was five minutes after six.

Mary opened the door. "Come in, please."

Kurt could feel eight pairs of eyes on him. Joey wasn't paying attention, and Little Sammy snuggled against his mother. Mary made the introductions.

"Hey, everyone, this is Kurt Kellerman. Kurt, you know Mom. This is my oldest brother, Bob, and his little girl, Lisa. This is my next oldest brother, Sam, his wife Nancy, and their baby, Little Sammy. I think you know my sister, Lori, and her husband, Terry Norris. And of course, here's my baby brother, Joey."

As she introduced each person, Kurt said hello and shook hands. It seemed a little overwhelming. Everyone was friendly except for Lori. She smiled and said hello, but her eyes shot daggers at Kurt. After the introductions, Mary and Kurt sat on the sofa beside one another.

Bob, Mary's oldest brother, was twenty-nine. He wore glasses and had black hair, male-pattern baldness, a Verdi beard, and a Dallas mustache. He was of medium height and neither overweight nor thin.

His daughter Lisa was two or three. Kurt wasn't a good judge of children's ages. She had straight, long blond hair and pretty blue eyes. Mary had told Kurt that Lisa was incredibly intelligent for her age.

Bob seemed to take charge and asked how many cars were needed. "We have eight adults and three children. I can take

Mom, Lisa, and Joey in my car. Can the rest of you squeeze into Sam's car?"

Sam said, "Nancy, Little Sammy, and I can ride in front. Lori, Terry, Mary, and Kurt can fit in the back." Everyone seemed to think this was all right. Kurt had no idea but was determined to be a team player. Everyone started heading out. They loaded up in a matter of minutes. Sam had a large Lincoln Continental. It was tight with four adults in the back, but not uncomfortable. Terry and Kurt sat by the doors.

Tonight was the second time that Kurt saw Mrs. Johnson. Most of the time she yelled at Mary and Kurt from her bedroom without coming out. She was heavy, with stooped shoulders, and had trouble moving around. Her eyes were dark brown and very alert. Her hair was dark brown, but it looked like she colored it, as some gray showed through. Her voice was loud and commanding. When she laughed, it was noisy and infectious. Kurt was surprised to find out she was only forty-six. She looked much older.

The drive to the pizza place was about twenty minutes. The conversation in Sam's car varied. It started with several questions about Little Sammy. Nancy passed some photos around. Kurt looked at the pictures.

"Little Sammy is cute. Those are nice."

Nancy retrieved the pictures. "Thank you, Kurt."

After ten minutes of talking about Little Sammy, Lori changed subjects. "I hear you're not a Catholic, Kurt. Is that right? You know that we are all Roman Catholic."

"Yes, I did know that Mary's family was Catholic. I'm a Baptist. I hope it isn't an issue for you."

"I just wanted to check. Mom was asking about it, and she seemed worried. I told her I'd find out."

"I'm pretty much an open book. You can ask me anything you like. I was curious: you, Terry, Sam, and Nancy are all out of school. What do you do?"

Sam spoke right up. He was twenty-two. He had a round face with dark eyes. Sam was a little plump. He liked to be well-dressed and wore expensive clothes.

"Nancy and I work together to run the Sears Store. We're the owner/franchise holders. We love it. Things are going very well. We're busy running the store and caring for Little Sammy."

Nancy was very pretty, with light brown hair and hazel eyes. She had a round face but was slim. Little Sammy was four months old. He was a chubby baby with big cheeks, a cute smile, and wisps of light hair. His mother had already got back into shape.

Terry answered next. He was short and thin, with a scruffy light brown beard and wavy light brown hair. He had rosy cheeks and seemed to always smile. It was rare to see him in anything other than blue jeans, a T-shirt or a checked, long-sleeved cotton shirt, and sneakers.

"I'm a civil engineer for the Kentucky Transportation Cabinet. I just started last year. Lori graduated from high school, and I graduated from college. I'm still new to everything, but we will make a nice living."

Lori had long, straight light brown hair parted in the middle, reaching halfway down her back. She was skinny, probably five feet two inches. She usually wore blue jeans but tended toward brightly colored blouses. Lori had an oval face with green eyes.

Kurt laughed. "My brother is a civil engineer for MODOT, the Missouri Department of Transportation. He loves it and seems to be doing well."

Lori leaned forward and looked directly at Kurt. Her arms were crossed. She wasn't smiling. "You're a senior in high school. What are your plans after you graduate?"

"I'm not positive, but everyone seems to be pushing me to study accounting and become a CPA. I'm not convinced it's right for me, but that is the plan for now."

"You're in luck, Kurt," said Sam. "Bob is a CPA. He studied

at the University of Illinois, passed his exams in one try, and got a nice job with a big company in Indianapolis. He can tell you everything you want to know about it and a lot of what you don't want to know. He loves it. He can talk about it for hours. Bores you to death."

They arrived at the pizza place, parked, and went inside. It was a little busy, but not terribly. There was about a ten-minute wait to get a large enough table for the group. The hostess seated them. Kurt sat beside Mary and across from Bob.

The server took everyone's drink requests. Bob was the life of the party while they were waiting. When she returned to take their meal orders, Bob ordered first. "I'll take a trip to the salad bar and a lovely pepperoni and cheese pizza for my daughter and me. I'm also paying for my mom, the older lady at the other end of the table. Can I take my trip now?"

Everyone laughed at Bob's playful banter, including the server. Kurt ordered a supreme pizza and a small cheese pizza for Joey. Mary wanted a salad, too, so that was added to Kurt's order. He had no idea as to what anyone else was doing. He was enjoying himself, other than the hostility that Lori seemed to be showing. Kurt figured he just needed to take it in stride, and it would go away.

He did notice Bob asking a lot of probing questions as well, but they weren't asked with an edge like Lori's. He asked what schools Kurt was considering, his career plans, and how football practice was going. Then Bob said he'd heard Kurt had helped Mary with some babysitting and wanted to know what he thought of that. Kurt said he enjoyed it. The food was good, and everyone seemed to be enjoying the meal. Finally, everyone finished, and it was time to leave.

The skating rink was around ten minutes away. They loaded up the same way as before. Mrs. Johnson and Nancy watched the three children. Everyone else skated. Here came the part that Kurt dreaded. Mary skated like she was made for it. Lori did as well. The others were not nearly as good but better than Kurt. Mary helped Kurt after she saw how badly he was struggling.

She took him by the hand and guided him around the rink for several laps. "I know you're good at this," he said. "Go ahead and have some fun skating fast if you'd like. I'll be okay."

Mary smiled. "I'm having fun teaching you. Just hold my hand."

The truth was, Kurt much preferred her hand and help to flailing around, barely able to keep his feet. After a while, they took a break to get a Coke.

As soon as they sat, Lisa and Joey swarmed Mary. Kurt was inexperienced with young children. His siblings had no children, and Kurt was the youngest in his family. Never having been around small children, he had no idea what to do. He ended up just trying to talk with them. After a few minutes, Lisa responded to Kurt's efforts. She shared with him that her favorite toy was "Bear" (her teddy bear). She also showed him the toy Grandma had gotten her from the vending machine. It was a plastic ring. She was very proud of it and was very excited to have jewelry. Joey had gotten a ball from the vending machine, and he wanted to bounce it back and forth with Kurt.

Nancy came by with Little Sammy. "Can you watch him while I go to the restroom and get a Coke?"

"Sure, I'm happy to. Take your time."

Children seemed to take to Mary quite naturally. After a few moments, Mary turned to Kurt. "Would you like to hold Little Sammy? He's an adorable baby."

In the pit of his stomach, Kurt believed this was a disaster in the making. He didn't even know how to hold a baby. However, he didn't want to refuse either.

"Sure, but you'll have to show me how to hold a baby."

Mary placed the baby in Kurt's arms. She told Kurt to support the baby's head and neck with one arm and his body with the other. Kurt hoped the trembling of his hands was not as apparent to Mary or anyone else as it was to him. He was terrified. Mary suggested he talk to Little Sammy to put the baby at ease. Kurt didn't know what to say to a child only a few months old, but he tried.

"Hello, Little Sammy. How are you doing, little man?" There. He'd talked to the baby. His conversation was all used up. What else could you say to an infant? Just then, Little Sammy reached up and grabbed Kurt's glasses. Before he knew what had happened, Little Sammy had clutched the eyewear like a prize. He waved them around for everyone to see, never taking his eyes off them.

From out of nowhere, Kurt said, "Hey! Do you like my glasses? You have pretty quick hands. How did you do that? Can I have my glasses back?"

Kurt then pulled on his glasses. It took two or three tries before he got them away from Little Sammy. They spent several minutes playing a game in which Little Sammy tried and sometimes succeeded in grabbing Kurt's glasses. Kurt was enjoying himself and bantered away to Little Sammy. After several minutes, Kurt realized he was ignoring Mary and looked up. Mary and Nancy both watched him with smiles.

Mary said, "I thought you weren't comfortable with babies. But you've taken up with Little Sammy. When Nancy came back, we didn't want to disturb you."

Kurt felt a little embarrassed. He blushed. He had enjoyed holding and playing with Little Sammy. "I suppose when he grabbed my glasses, I quit worrying about what to do and just started playing with him. I was so busy with him that I lost track of everything else. I've never held a baby before, but Little Sammy is all right."

Nancy took her son back from Kurt, saying he needed a feeding. Mary continued to sit and smile at Kurt. Her mother was also watching everything that happened.

Kurt asked Mary if she wanted to skate some more. They did

this for around fifteen minutes before it was time to go. Instead of zipping around like she could, Mary was content to hold Kurt's hand and guide him around. He looked at her. *I've never enjoyed skating in my life. I always hated it. But it's so nice being here with Mary. Even watching the kids with her is great. It's being with Mary that makes everything good. I wonder if this is what it's like to be in love.*

On the drive home, everyone was in high spirits. Some commented that Bob and Kurt looked uncomfortable on skates, which everyone laughed at. Terry asked what the plans were for Saturday. Several possibilities were thrown out, but nothing was decided. Then Nancy told everyone about Kurt holding and playing with Little Sammy.

Lori asked, "Do you like babies, Kurt?"

Kurt turned a little red but hoped no one could see it. "I don't know if I like babies or not. I like Little Sammy. When he grabbed my glasses and then kept playing tug-of-war with them, it was just—well, it was just sweet. I've never been around a baby in my life. When he smiles at you, I don't know how you couldn't like him."

"Do you plan on having children someday?"

Everyone in the car shouted, "Lori!"

But Kurt answered, "I suppose I've always assumed one of these days I would get married and have three or four children. But that's for somewhere way down the road. It might be that I came from a family of five, which seems natural to me. But the answer is yes."

That killed the conversation for a minute. Nancy broke the silence by saying, "How fast are you driving, Sam?"

"Seventy-five."

"But the speed limit is fifty-five. The last thing we need is to pay for a ticket for speeding. Slow down."

Everyone laughed, and then the conversation picked up again. Most was about what everyone was doing over the next few weeks. It appeared the Johnson family got together regularly. This was new to Kurt. His siblings came home two or three times yearly, and his parents visited them once or twice yearly. He was interested in the inner workings. *It seems odd that Nancy sounded so worried about a speeding ticket. They own a successful business. He drives an expensive car.* Kurt stopped worrying and enjoyed the evening.

When they got home, everyone went inside except Mary and Kurt. Mary said, "Did you have an okay time? I know Lori pushed you a little. Plus, it was clear that roller-skating is something you haven't done very often."

"I had a wonderful time! It was the best time I've ever had on roller skates. Your brother Bob is nice and pretty funny. Nancy is super sweet. Sam and Terry are both entertaining. I enjoyed Little Sammy, Lisa, and Joey. That was the happiest and most relaxed I've ever seen your mother. I've known Lori since I started high school. She has strong opinions and still resents me being here when she brought a date for you. That's no big deal, and she'll get over it. But most of all, I like being with you."

"Can you come over tomorrow? It will still be the whole family again."

"Just let me know what time, and I'll be here."

"Plan on after lunch. Probably around one o'clock. If it changes, I'll call."

Kurt nodded, and they kissed each other good night. She went into the house. He drove home and pondered the evening. A part of him had been worried he would be bored or embarrassed. Especially when he found out roller-skating was on the agenda. Yet he had truly enjoyed the entire evening. Unlike his family, Mary's was fun and full of life. While all those things were nice, the main thing was Mary herself. When she smiled at him, it melted his heart. Her brown eyes were just the right shade to match her complexion and hair. She was so kind and sweet, and he couldn't find the words to describe her many perfections. All Kurt knew was that he wanted to be with her as much as possible.

After a long, hard week, Kurt was exhausted. It took a little while to fall asleep because he had so many things running through his head, but he dozed off. He didn't wake up until around 10:15 the next morning. He got dressed and then had his favorite breakfast of peanut butter on toast and Nestle's Quik. There were no calls from Mary, so he headed to her house at ten minutes till one. He parked in front of the house about three minutes early. As he went up the steps, the door opened, and Terry invited him into the house. Mary and Lori were finishing cleaning up the lunch dishes. Kurt sat on the sofa.

The house filled with chatter. Joey and Lisa were playing together on the floor. Mrs. Johnson and Nancy sat at the kitchen table with Little Sammy. Bob, Terry, and Sam were in the living room with Kurt. After Kurt sat down, Terry leaned over.

"So, just how sore are you today from skating, or maybe I should say trying to skate?" Everyone laughed, including Kurt.

"I think I'm sorer from roller-skating than I've ever been from football." Again, everyone had a good laugh.

Bob spoke up. "As long as we're having Grilled Kurt today, did you enjoy Lori's questions last night?"

"I didn't feel like I was being grilled. I know Lori. She had questions, and she wanted answers. Asking the questions is a pretty good way to resolve that dilemma. So what are we doing this afternoon?"

Bob said, "Terry and Lori will visit his parents for a while. They'll be back for dinner. We'll take it easy and stay around the house visiting."

They started swapping childhood stories. They also shared things they were doing or planning to do soon. There was a lot of playful banter that went on all afternoon. Bob and Sam went outside to take care of something in the backyard their mother had asked them to fix.

That evening, after dinner, they all gathered again. Little Sammy reached for Kurt, so Kurt took him. Once again, a contest was on for control of Kurt's glasses. He and Little Sammy went on for perhaps fifteen minutes before Little Sammy decided he wanted his mother. Kurt had enjoyed Little Sammy.

At one point, the subject of religion came up. Lori asked Kurt where he went to church. Kurt answered that he attended a small Baptist church in the country.

Lori asked, "How often do you go to your church?"

"Sunday morning and Sunday evening, every week."

"Do you ever go for holy days or special services?"

"We're having revival services in a few weeks. We'll meet every night for at least a week and possibly longer. I won't go on Friday nights because of football games, but I'll go to the rest of it."

"Is there anything special about it?" Lori asked.

"Well, instead of the pastor, there will be a guest speaker, and instead of our regular music, there will be a family that travels around doing music at a lot of churches in the area."

Lori rolled her eyes. "Who are these special people?"

"The speaker is a former Marine. He was wounded in Vietnam and lost both legs when a land mine went off. He's a very popular speaker and will be there every night. His name is Tim Lee. The musicians are a family whose last name starts with an S. I never can remember their names. It's a husband and wife with a daughter a little younger than me. They live about thirty miles from here."

Mary and her mother both started talking at once. Mrs. Johnson took the floor. "I like Tim Lee. He spoke at Lori's high school graduation and did a wonderful job. I enjoy hearing him speak."

Mary spoke up. "Would the musicians be the Shelton family?"

"Maybe. I'm not sure," Kurt answered.

Mary asked, "Does the daughter have a gold tooth?"

Kurt's mouth dropped open. "Yes, she does. How did you know?"

"They were our neighbors before Dad died. She got the gold tooth playing with me one day. We were both acting silly, spinning around and around. She got dizzy and fell and broke a tooth. I haven't seen her since we moved away."

"Would you want to go to the revival services with me and see her?" Kurt asked.

There was a moment of silence. Mary and Lori both looked at their mother. Mrs. Johnson said, "If I permit Mary to attend your church, would you be willing to attend Mass with her?"

Kurt said, "That seems only fair. Sure, I would be happy to do that. Thank you. There's only one thing. Mary, do you want to do this? I know you expressed that she was your friend, and you haven't seen her in a long time, but you're not obligated to go. I was extending the invitation if you wanted to."

Mary said, "I think it would be great. Thank you. And thank you, Mom."

It seemed as if a lot of tension had left the air at this point. Of course, Kurt had no idea how his parents would react to what he'd done. But he'd figure it out. Meanwhile, things had lightened up a great deal, and Lori seemed a little less hostile.

When Kurt left that evening, he asked Mary, "Is everything okay? I didn't mean to put you on the spot. I was answering questions. You don't have to go to church with me if you don't want to."

"Everything is great. I know Mom and Lori have been talking about this a lot. I've dated other boys who weren't Catholic, but they weren't anything. They didn't go to church. Most of the boys I've dated were Catholic, but not many of them attend church either. I wasn't worried about it, but Mom and Lori talked about nothing else. It helped that they both liked Tim Lee and the Sheltons. Everyone is leaving tomorrow morning. Is there any chance you could come over tomorrow afternoon or evening? We don't have school Monday. It's Labor Day."

"I can come over tomorrow afternoon. I'll do my best to make it stretch into tomorrow evening. Do you want to go anywhere?"

"No. I think it would be nice to spend some time alone together."

They said good night as Kurt wrapped his arms around Mary. They kissed. She went back into the house. Kurt got in his car and drove home as if in a dream. Everything about her was perfect. He knew the religious issues had been at least part of the problem with her family, but that appeared to be resolved tonight. Things couldn't be better. Again, he dropped off into a deep sleep.

Chapter 4
September 1974

The Perfect Day

Sunday morning came early for Kurt. He rolled out of bed, had breakfast, and dressed for church. Kurt was usually attentive at church, but his mind was elsewhere this Sunday. He couldn't wait to get home and head over to see Mary. It seemed like the worship service dragged on forever. When he got home, he changed clothes and came to Sunday dinner. His mother fixed a pot roast on Sunday. It was one of his favorite meals, but he got smaller than usual servings this Sunday and gulped down his food.

As he headed out the door, he shouted, "I'm probably going to spend the rest of the day at Mary's! Goodbye!" Kurt hurried out toward his car.

The back door swung open, and his father said, "What time will you be home?"

Kurt stopped. He turned to face his father. "Well, there's no school tomorrow. I thought around eleven or twelve o'clock. Is that all right?"

After a pause, his father said, "That's fine. I just wanted to know."

When Kurt got to Mary's house, he parked in front, on the street. He exited the car, ran to the door, and knocked. The door swung open, and there was Mary with her special smile. He came in and took his usual place on the sofa.

"Where is everyone?"

"They've all gone home. Joey wanted to spend the night with Sam and Nancy, so he's gone too. Mom is back in her room. She's exhausted from being up with everyone all weekend and going out on Friday night."

"What would you like to do today, Mary?"

"I thought we could sit and talk. Maybe listen to some records. Just have some peace and quiet."

She turned on a record album and sat by Kurt. They held hands and looked at one another. Then they kissed. It was long and slow, followed by more. She leaned her head on his shoulder. He wrapped his arm around her.

Kurt announced, "I have a question for you. What did your family think of me? It was obvious they were checking me out all weekend."

"They like you. Lori and Mom have been all hung up over the Catholic–Baptist thing. They can tell you are serious about where you go to church. Besides everything we've already mentioned, Bob brought something up at breakfast. No one in our family goes to Mass very often except me. So he didn't see why it bothered them so much which church you went to. Bob's smart like that.

"Bob and Sam liked you a lot. They thought the way you got on well with Joey, Lisa, and Little Sammy was great. Nancy liked you too. I don't think Terry cares who I date. Mom and Lori are the difficult ones. Oh, and Mom never likes anyone I date. So I think things went well."

Kurt saw her brown eyes searching and penetrating his very

soul. They were watching his face, taking in his reaction. Again, he leaned over and kissed her.

"For whatever it's worth, I liked all of them. They're a lot more fun than my family. I still can't believe we all went roller-skating Friday night. My family would never do that."

Mary smiled. "I'm glad everything went well. Whenever Lori started talking, I was on pins and needles, especially when she asked if you wanted to have children someday."

Kurt shrugged. "That was a little awkward, but everyone had the same reaction. I guess she has us married off already."

"The funny thing is that when she said that, it sealed your approval by everyone else. There was a discussion this morning about how insane that question was. Even Terry told her she was a psycho, and he never stands up to Lori. Bob and Mom were shocked when they heard it. Bob said that if you still wanted to go out with me after that, it must mean you liked me a lot. He said he would have been looking for the closest exit after something like that."

Their conversation turned to gossip about friends and school. The subject of family had been discussed. It was a pretty day, and they went for a drive. Nothing exciting happened. Kurt drove out into the country on some old roads and pointed out places he thought were pretty or where he could tell some story from his childhood.

Kurt asked Mary to tell him more about her childhood. She talked about where she'd started school. Her father's death. It was clear that she adored and missed him. She described moving to a new community. One of the things that helped her meet people was playing in the band. The school band was very popular, and many students participated. It was a good way to meet people. Her first boyfriend had been the only boy in the French horn section. As time passed, she met more and more people and felt at home.

When they returned to Mary's house, they had leftovers for

their evening meal. Mary served her mother, who was still in her bedroom. After eating, they washed and dried the dishes. Then they entered the living room and sat beside one another on the sofa.

"We've talked about me and my family. So tell me about yourself."

This was hard for him to do. "I don't know. I like that my name means polite or courteous. I try to be that. I'm a little vain about my intelligence. I have a high IQ, but sometimes I'm arrogant and come off as a know-it-all. I wouldn't say I like it, but I know it's true. Oh, and I'm crazy about you."

That was Kurt's description of himself. He wasn't sure if it was accurate or not. But he believed it was as close to the truth as possible. He asked Mary what she thought of his self-description.

Again, she smiled her special smile. "I can tell you that I think you're very attractive. So you can check that off. I must admit that in the past you have come off as something of a know-it-all, or as you said, arrogant. But if a person gets to know you, she would realize that's not quite right. You are VERY confident that what you think is true. But you are probably the nicest guy I've ever met. That means a lot to me. I've dated far too many guys who weren't nice."

"I hope you can put up with my being a know-it-all. I need to work on it, but that won't be easy."

Mary smiled. "I think I can deal with it."

Kurt drew Mary closer. She tilted her head back, and he leaned toward her. They kissed. It was long and gentle. She wrapped her arms around him. They kissed again and again. They were lost in one another. There was no one and nothing else in the world but the two of them.

Later, Mary turned on the television, and they watched it for a few hours. Then Kurt asked a question. "Have all of your boyfriends met your family?"

"No. Most of them haven't met my family other than Joey and Mom. Some of them met or knew Lori, just like you. The only one I can think of who met the rest of the family was Tommy English. We were dating when I turned sixteen, and everyone came home for my birthday. That reminds me, why you didn't stay long at my birthday party? You were there. I remember. But you left quickly. Weren't you enjoying it?"

"I did go. But in all honesty, I was a little jealous watching you and Tommy English dancing together. I don't know how to dance. I was very attracted to you. Tommy is one of my friends. He's a lot of the things I'm not. He's popular. He's a good dancer. He's gone out with lots of girls. It was just better for me to leave."

Mary laughed. "Tommy may be a lot of things that you are not, but you are a lot of things that he is not. I love to dance, and I'd love to teach you to dance."

Kurt blushed. "You don't know how clumsy I am. Teaching me to dance might be more than you're bargaining for. What would you like to do tomorrow?"

"Today was nice. Why don't we do the same thing tomorrow? Maybe you could bring a few of your favorite albums and let me listen to them."

It was time for Kurt to go home. They got up and walked to the door. He kissed Mary good night and left.

Kurt got up the next morning, had breakfast, and read the morning paper. It was raining, so his father went uptown to one of the local cafés to drink coffee with his friends. His mother talked on the phone with one of her friends. She loved doing this. When she hung up the phone, she walked into where Kurt was sitting.

"So, how is everything going? We haven't seen much of you lately."

"Everything is great. I'm enjoying football. My classes seem all right. I'm enjoying dating Mary."

The wrinkles on Mrs. Kellerman's forehead showed. "You're seeing a lot of her."

"Yes. She's far and away the nicest girl I've ever gone out with. Her family is nice. I'm the happiest I've been since I started high school."

"We don't know much about her or her family."

What's going on here? She sounds like Lori. Mom and Dad have never asked me about any other girls I've dated. He decided to be as upfront with his mother as with Lori.

"What do you want to know? No one's hiding anything. How about if I bring her to the revival services one night?"

"That would be nice. Do you think she'll come?"

"She's already said yes! Her mother says it's all right for her to go! Any other questions or problems?" Kurt was angry. He was bouncing his leg under the table. It was making the room shake.

"There aren't any problems. We didn't know much about her."

"I'm going to her house after lunch to spend the rest of the day with her. I'll see you later tonight." Kurt didn't wait for his mother to fix lunch. He made himself a sandwich and ate it. Then he left with two or three of his favorite albums. He drove around and stopped by to see Racket. Racket worked at a service station on the edge of town. Pete was there too. The three friends chatted for a little while. When ten minutes till one rolled around, Kurt said goodbye and drove to Mary's.

When he arrived, the rain was pouring harder than it had all day. The temperature dropped. Kurt parked on the street, grabbed the records, and ran as fast as possible to the door. He knocked and waited. Meanwhile, he was getting soaked to the bone with large, icy raindrops. The door opened, and there was Mary, pretty as ever. She was looking at the equivalent of a five-foot, eleven-inch drowning rat. He came in, and Mary greeted him with a kiss.

"You'll get soaking wet!" he warned her.

"I don't care!" She kissed him again and hugged him. He held her tight.

Mary got some towels so they could dry off. She went to her bedroom and changed her blouse. They sat together on the sofa after they were both dry (Kurt was still a little damp). He showed her the albums he brought. She asked him to pick one to play. That was easy. He chose Don McLean's *American Pie* album, the A-side.

Mary put it on the turntable, and it began to play "American Pie." They both enjoyed the song. As it was ending, Kurt spoke up. "Would you like to dance to the next two or three songs? I'm not very good at it, but slow dancing is easier than fast. Remember, I don't offer to dance very often."

"Of course." She stood. Took his hand. She looked into his eyes with her beautiful brown eyes and stood close to him.

The next song was a short number called "Till Tomorrow." They held one another close and swayed to the music. Kurt didn't know what he was doing, but he knew he was doing it with Mary. The music was soft and low. The rain beat down on the roof and the windows. They were all alone in their own little world. The next song was "Vincent." Finally, the album ended with "Crossroads."

It was the most Kurt had ever danced. From beginning to end, they shuffled their feet and swayed in rhythm to the music. Her head was on his shoulder, and his head leaned down against her. Occasionally, their eyes would meet. Hers a penetrating medium brown; his a twinkling bright blue. Kurt could feel Mary's heart beating against his. It was difficult for him to tell where her body ended and his began. They were one. Why had he never wanted to dance? It was wonderful. After the record ended, they sat on the sofa again.

Even though Kurt exploded with happiness, he asked Mary,

"Was that all right? Did I step on you? Did I do things wrong? I don't know how to do this."

Mary smiled. If possible, Kurt grew even happier. "That was great," she said. "Who told you that you didn't know how to dance?"

"I don't know if anyone told me. I think I just assumed it."

"Well, you assumed wrong."

They leaned toward one another and kissed, holding each other tight. They kissed again, again, and again. After a while, Mary stood. "I've got to do something in the kitchen. Could you put on another album?" Kurt chose a Crosby, Stills, Nash, and Young album. It started playing while Mary was still in the kitchen. Kurt wasn't sure about trying to dance to this album. He did ask Mary what she had to do in the kitchen. She told him it was a surprise and he would have to figure it out. A few minutes later, the song "Our House" played, and once again, they got up and danced. When the song was over, Kurt realized what was going on.

"You're baking cookies!"

"Yes, I am, and I'd better go check them."

A few minutes later, he heard her take some cookies back to her mother. Then she brought a plate of cookies and two glasses of milk into the living room. She grabbed a blanket that was nearby and threw it over them. They sat and ate, drank milk, heard the last song or two on the album, and then listened to the rain. When they finished the cookies, they again enclosed one another in their arms and kissed. She filled him with desires that no one else ever had. Yet he did not want to do anything that might damage their relationship. It took every bit of his willpower not to cross the line.

After a while, they decided to listen to *American Pie* again. They got up and danced through the entire A-side of the album. Kurt never forgot that afternoon for the rest of his life. He never forgot that their first dance was to "Till Tomorrow." Kurt never heard those songs again without being reminded of that beautiful Labor Day.

Mary fried some chicken and cooked mashed potatoes and corn for dinner. Again, they washed and dried together. The food was delicious. As much as Kurt hated it, he had football practice at six that night. He waited until the last possible minute, then kissed Mary goodbye and left.

The rain had changed to sleet. During practice, it changed again to snow. Nothing stuck to the ground because of the rain, and the temperature drop had been very sudden. After practice was over, Kurt reflected on his day. *I should have skipped practice and stayed with Mary. It would have meant a lot of additional sprints and laps, but it would have been worth it. I can't believe I left to come here.* But Kurt obeyed authority. Even when he later regretted it. But forever in his heart and mind, Labor Day was the Perfect Day as far as Kurt was concerned.

Years later, Kurt still considered that afternoon the happiest day of his life. He listens to the music, listens to the rain, and eats freshly baked cookies. He kisses Mary, dances with her, holds her in his arms, stares into her eyes, sees her smile up at him, and feels her heartbeat as they hold each other close. Yes, that was indeed the happiest day of his life.

Getting to Know One Another

For the rest of September, Kurt and Mary spent as much time together as possible. They met before school started, and he walked her to most of her classes. After school, he went to football practice but called her when he got home. On Friday nights, Kurt started and played the varsity football game. If it was a home game, he would go to Mary's house afterward. Sometimes it was too late to get together when he returned to town on the team bus. They spent the day together on Saturday and again on Sunday afternoon.

There were a few variations that occurred. The revival services at Kurt's church began, and Mary came with him. She enjoyed seeing her old friend singing at Kurt's church. As promised, Kurt went to Mass with Mary on Saturday evening. He'd never been to a Catholic church before, so the service there was as strange to Kurt as the service at his church had been to Mary. But being together was the important thing. Mary's mother permitted Mary to attend several of the services with Kurt. So they went at every opportunity.

Kurt told his parents he was attending Saturday evening Mass with Mary. He knew they would hear it from local gossip in their small town and figured it was best to be up-front about it. Mrs. Kellerman looked at Kurt. "Why on earth are you going to Mass at a Catholic church?" She was upset.

"I promised Mrs. Johnson that if Mary came to church with me, I would attend Saturday night Mass with Mary. She's already been to our church three or four times. I think I can deal with going to one Mass." This appeared to be all right with them, and he didn't bring it up again.

The two of them were glad to have reasons to see one another. It helped them get to know each other better as they discussed their beliefs. Mary had several questions about what she heard at Kurt's church, and he peppered her with questions about Catholicism. Each had deeply held beliefs. Both respected the other's beliefs and were eager to learn about them.

Another out-of-the-ordinary routine was that Kurt took Mary to some out-of-town freshman football games. Varsity practice let out early on Thursdays. Kurt picked up Mary, and they got a burger at a drive-in before the game.

What surprised Kurt was that he didn't care about watching the game when Mary was with him. He spent the whole time talking with her. After a pleasant drive home, he walked her to the door and said good night. He didn't leave until she was inside with the door shut.

Kurt had been obsessed with football for years, but it wasn't important. If he could take Mary to a game, it was just a weeknight date. After Mass on Saturday nights, they would catch a movie. Usually, they went to a drive-in theater. Sometimes they watched the film; some nights they didn't.

Kurt and Mary discussed politics, race, religion, and other topics. He loved that she wasn't afraid to disagree with him. With her sweet presentation of her ideas, Kurt reconsidered some of his. No one had ever been able to change Kurt's mind before, but Mary could. She was slowly chipping away at his arrogance.

One weekend, Lori and Terry were home. Kurt braced himself for potential battles with Lori. Things went better than expected. Lori found a souvenir book from a Three Dog Night concert that Terry had taken her to when they were dating. She enjoyed the trip through memory lane. Kurt was interested in looking at the photo album. He was a fan of Three Dog Night too. Finally, Kurt and Lori agreed on something! It seemed to break down the walls a little further.

One evening, Mrs. Kellerman had a question for Kurt. "Do you think Mary would want to ride with us to your game Friday?"

"I don't know, but I'll ask her and let you know." Kurt chose not to mention it to Mary on the telephone that evening. It seemed to him it would be better to ask her in person. He thought it might be very awkward for her and wanted Mary to have every opportunity to wiggle out of it. Kurt even started thinking up excuses for her.

The next day, during study hall, he brought it up. "Mary, my parents wanted to know if you would like to ride to the game Friday night with them. If you don't want to, that's fine. There's no pressure."

"I'd love to. That will give me a chance to get to know them better. Is it okay if I call your mother and talk to her about it?"

"Sure. That would be great."

When he got home from practice that night, his mom said, "I got a phone call from Mary this afternoon. She's going to ride with us to your game. She seemed happy to come with us. I think she's a sweet girl." After that, Mary rode with Kurt's parents to all his out-of-town games.

Kurt and Mary got to know each other much better. They began to learn one another's quirks. Also, each became pretty familiar with the other's likes and dislikes. For instance, while Mary liked rock and roll music, she also liked country and the new Southern or country rock genre. Kurt had quit listening to country music when he became a teenager, but due to Mary's influence, he began to enjoy it again.

Another area that showed up was Kurt's relationship with Joey. Kurt thought of himself as a big brother/babysitter to Joey, as he assisted in babysitting Joey. But Joey did not accept that relationship. His favorite words to Kurt were, "You're not the boss of me." Kurt realized he pushed too hard and needed to befriend Joey. Joey was a little boy with no father. He wanted a male to relate to but considered Kurt nothing more than Mary's boyfriend, who would be around a couple of months and then be gone. Mary seemed to understand the situation and helped Kurt and Joey navigate some tricky waters.

Kurt gained an appreciation for how responsible Mary was. She cared for her ailing mother and baby brother, did most of the cooking, laundry, and housework, and went to school. He had no idea how she did all of that. Kurt did his best to assist Mary in many of these responsibilities. He wasn't sure how much he helped, but Mary seemed to appreciate his efforts.

Mary, her mother, and Joey lived off social security benefits from her deceased father. Mary had a lot to do with managing the household finances. They received help from her older siblings, particularly her oldest brother, Bob. Kurt tried to ensure he didn't do things that increased the Johnsons' expenses, such as eating at their house.

Mary learned Kurt was more sensitive than she first thought. Much of his talking and a lot of his joking was designed to cover up his insecurities. She seemed to be able to look at him and read his mind.

On the other hand, for all her sweetness, there was a tough edge to Mary. She had to have this to take care of all the responsibilities she was faced with at such a young age. She had essentially run the household from the age of fourteen. People had tried to take advantage of her, and some had succeeded. She had developed that toughness out of necessity. When she felt disrespected, lied to, or taken advantage of, she could be very determined to fight it.

Kurt stopped by after football practice one night. It was pouring rain. He wanted to surprise Mary with a small gift, some earrings he thought she would like. He knocked on the door, and Mary opened it.

"Come in. I wasn't expecting to see you." She kissed him and smiled. "What's going on?"

"I just wanted to give you a little surprise. It's the one-month anniversary of the first time I made Lori mad." He held out the small box. She looked down at it, smiling. Suddenly, the smile disappeared. "What are you doing, tracking all that mud in here!"

Kurt was shocked. Mary had never said an angry word to him. He looked down and saw that his shoes were covered in mud, and he'd got it all over the floor near the front door. "I'm sorry. I didn't realize there was mud on my shoes. I'll clean it up right now." He started to take a step to get something to clean with but stopped when he heard Mary shout.

"Don't move! You'll make it worse. I spent nearly two hours

cleaning all the floors last night." Tears were streaming down her face.

Kurt took his shoes off and went to get some things to clean the floor. Mary calmed down. She looked at him scrubbing the floor and giggled. "You don't even know what you're doing. I'll show you how to do it." She started scrubbing, and they cleaned the floor together.

Kurt kept apologizing. All the while, he was thinking *I've blown it. Here I meant to make her happy, and I've just added to all the work she has to do. She's probably going to tell me to leave and not come back. I wouldn't blame her if she did, but I couldn't handle it.*

"I'm sorry I lost it. It's just that I spend so much time caring for Mom and Joey, doing all the laundry, and cleaning the house. I never get any help. Well, not often. You've helped me with the dishes a few times. I worked so hard yesterday that I freaked out when I saw all that mud."

"You don't have anything to be sorry about. I'm sorry I made things harder for you. I'm amazed at all your responsibilities and the work you do, and you still make time for me. That was why I wanted to surprise you tonight."

The mess was clean now. They got up and put away their cleaning supplies.

Mary smiled as she picked up the box Kurt had handed her. She opened it to find earrings that matched one of her favorite necklaces. "They're beautiful. Thank you for being so sweet."

"Thank you for being the most amazing person I've ever known. I don't know how you do it all. If you need help with anything, please ask me. I want to help you, not make life harder."

Mary was late for study hall on Tuesday. Kurt wasn't sure what was happening, so he sat with Tommy English, Rudy, and a few other friends at a table.

Rudy asked, "Tommy, who are you taking out? I heard you broke up with Emily Snicker."

"Well, I know what I want out of a girl. It was pretty good while I was seeing Mary Johnson. I liked what I got, but it was time for something different. Emily put out too. But I got tired of her faster than I did Mary. I asked Lana Childers out. Everyone says she's a wild woman."

Most of the guys laughed. Someone said, "You're the man, Tommy." But Kurt was uncomfortable. He thought, *No, I'm mad. Mary's not that kind of girl. He needs to shut up.* Kurt stood up. Mary was standing there beside him! She was not smiling. Her eyes flashed fire. "Tommy, I need to talk to you. Now!"

Tommy stood up and went to a table alone with Mary. "How dare you say those things about me! Heaven knows you tried to get what you wanted from me. But if memory serves me correctly, you never got anywhere with that. You broke up with me because you thought Emily would give you what you wanted. Am I missing something?"

"Um, no! I didn't mean anything by that. I was bragging to the guys. You know how it is. Nobody believes that stuff."

Mary's eyes still blazed. Her mouth was so thin it looked like a short, straight line.

"No! I don't know how it is with guys. I can tell you this. You know I'm dating Kurt Kellerman. Some people have asked me why. Now I know what to tell them. I'm dating Kurt because he's nothing at all like you! I never expected to hear you telling anyone what you got from me was 'pretty good.' You got nothing from me. And you never will! Now get up and leave."

After Tommy went back to his table, Kurt sat down with Mary. "I'm sorry you had to hear that. I was so angry that I stood up to do something. I think I was getting ready to punch Tommy. You handled it pretty well."

Mary's eyes glistened with tears. Kurt thought they were from a mixture of sadness and anger.

"Thank you. When I walked in, I was happy and looked forward to sitting with you. When I came to the table, I heard

Tommy. I watched in disbelief. I saw you get up. But I wanted to handle it myself. He won't be talking about me anymore. I've learned how to take care of his kind. It's part of why I'm so happy to be with you."

Kurt hugged Mary. Mrs. Grant, Kurt's least favorite teacher ever, came walking by. "None of that in here! This is a study hall! Get your books out and keep your hands to yourself, Kellerman!"

Mary looked up, and again, her eyes showed nothing but anger. "Mrs. Grant, Tommy English said some horrible things to me. Kurt defended me and gave me a hug to comfort me. I understand that isn't what study hall is for, but I needed someone to do that."

Kurt was naive. Mary was not. She had to deal with issues that Kurt never dreamed of facing. His parents cared for the family and household, but no one cared for Mary. She respected her mother and family but was willing to stand up to them.

Kurt was seven months older but didn't consider disobeying his parents. That was one of the ways he was also different from his sister and brother. They were both more rebellious. They had rejected many of their parents' viewpoints and values, including the church. Kurt accepted his parents' authority even when he disagreed with it. If anything, Kurt exceeded their religious devotion.

He loved that Mary was going to church with him. He enjoyed going with her. But he was firmly committed to his personal Christian beliefs. Mary liked this about Kurt. It was an area in which he showed some authentic leadership. But he did it in a kind, gentle, understanding way. Many of the things where they differed were up for negotiation, but this was not one of them. Still, he enjoyed it when one day he found a book of childhood prayers she had as a young girl. He read them and talked with her about them. He asked questions. Kurt didn't make any negative comments. He showed respect for her beliefs and was trying to learn about them. But he would not adopt those with which he disagreed.

Most importantly, they loved being together and wanted to spend as much time together as possible. The Saturday night after Labor Day, he gave her his class ring to wear. She wore it constantly. Every day, they grew to know one another better.

That weekend was the annual Fall Festival. A carnival arrived. Local groups had contests, sometimes plays or other productions. On Saturday evening there would be a parade. There were all sorts of food stands.

On Thursday Kurt and Mary took Joey to the carnival so he could ride the rides. He had a great time. Kurt enjoyed watching Mary with Joey. She loved Joey and took excellent care of him.

Saturday night, they went for the parade. Mary was marching with the band. After the parade, Mary ran home and changed clothes. They walked around the festival, enjoying visiting with everyone they met. After a while, Mary said she was ready to go home. Kurt took her, and they went to the house to watch television. Mary put Joey to bed, and then they sat on the sofa, talking low. September had been very busy. They knew one another so much better now than they had before.

Kurt asked Mary if she was happy. She answered, "I don't know when I've ever been happier. What about you?"

"Whenever we're together, I think I'm the happiest I've ever been. Then I see you again, and I'm happier still. I'm beginning to wonder just how filled with peace, joy, and happiness a person can be. I've never known anyone like you. I didn't know dating someone could be this wonderful. Most of my relationships have been a lot of work. I'm in love with you."

Mary smiled her special smile. "I've been waiting to hear those words from you. I love you too. I've known it since the night you met all my family. It's been so wonderful."

"I thought I loved you that night, but I wasn't sure. It was so quick. But I knew when we listened to the rain and the music and talked on Labor Day. When I asked you to dance with me, that was my way of telling you that I love you."

Mary laughed. "When I baked those chocolate chip cookies, it was my way of telling you that I love you."

They both smiled and rested in one another's arms. It had been another wonderful day. Another day of happiness. It seemed as though this would go on and on forever.

Chapter 5
October 1974

An Unexpected Trip

O ctober began with a surprise. When Kurt called Mary after football practice, she had some unexpected news. Her brother Bob had tickets for the Ringling Brothers Barnum and Bailey Circus on Sunday. He bought them for the entire family, plus Kurt. Everyone was invited to go to Indianapolis and stay with him for the weekend.

"Would you like to go? Bob said you're invited."

"I'd love to. I need to check on a couple of things first. Can I call you back in a few minutes?"

"Of course. I'll be waiting."

Kurt wanted to go without a doubt. He needed to resolve two issues. First, he needed his parents' permission. Second, he had a game on Friday night. He couldn't leave until after the game or on Saturday morning.

He walked into the family room where his parents were watching television.

"Mom, Dad, Mary asked me if I could go with her to visit her brother in Indianapolis. He's got tickets for the Ringling Brothers Circus. I'd like to go."

His mother and father looked at one another. She said, "Do you know her brother?"

"Yes. His name is Bob. He's a CPA with a large accounting firm in downtown Indianapolis."

"Well, Mary has been going to church with you, and she's been very nice when we took her to your football games. I guess it's all right." His father added, "I hope you have a good time."

Kurt ran to the other room and dialed as fast as he could. "Mary, I can go! There's only one problem. I can't leave until after the game Friday night. That's pretty late."

"We're going to leave early on Saturday morning. So that's not a problem. I'm glad you're coming."

So everything was set. The week flew by. The departure time for Saturday was 7:00 a.m. That meant Kurt would need to be up a little after 6:00. He packed an overnight bag and set his alarm. Sam and Nancy's car pulled up in front of the Kellerman house at 7:00 a.m. Kurt was ready. He said goodbye to his mother; his father had already gone to work. His bag was thrown in the trunk, and Kurt climbed into the back seat on the passenger side.

They took off, and the trip began. Sam, Mrs. Johnson, and Little Sammy were in the front seat. Nancy, Joey, Mary, and Kurt sat in the back. Everyone was excited to be going to Bob's home. He had a condominium on the west side of Indianapolis. Lori and Terry drove up separately. The interstates in the area were not yet completed, so they took two-lane highways for several hours and got on Interstate 70, a little west of Terre Haute.

Initially, the talk was about what Bob's home would be like. How much Joey and Lisa would enjoy the circus came next. Then it went in random directions. After about two-and-a-half hours, they stopped to buy gas and go to a restaurant for brunch. It was nothing special, but everyone was in high spirits and enjoyed the meal. The chatter continued through the meal. Before they went back to the car, Kurt took Joey to the bathroom.

"Joey, what do you think about going to the circus?"

"I want to see the lions. Them, and the tigers, and the guys who do tricks with them." He seemed like a delighted little boy.

After they got back in the car, sleepiness overtook Kurt. His body was very achy from the previous night's game. It was against the largest school in their conference. The largest school tended to have the largest players. This school had a six-foot-four-inch fullback who was one of the top two runners in the state in the one-hundred-yard dash and best in the state in the 220. Kurt had made around eight solo tackles on him and was still sore from it. His stomach full, he sat with his arm around Mary, who had already dozed off with her head on his shoulder. Within a few minutes, Kurt was asleep too.

A little while later, Kurt awakened. He blinked and stared out the window. He noticed the car they were going around had unusual license plates with a large five-point star in a circle.

"Is that car we're going around some kind of a sheriff or police officer?"

"Oh no!" Sam yelled. "I believe it's a policeman."

Somebody checked. Mrs. Johnson confirmed it was a police officer. Looking through his rearview mirror, Sam began to pull over on the shoulder as he saw the policeman turn on his siren and flashing lights.

"I was doing around eighty-five in a fifty-five. This is going to be expensive."

Kurt said, "This may not help, but Joey was looking out the back window and waving bye-bye as we passed him."

"I'm doomed!"

The police officer was very polite, but Sam did get a ticket for exceeding the speed limit by more than twenty miles per hour. He told Sam to slow down. The police officer also warned Sam that there were more police cars between wherever we were and Indianapolis. The last hour of the trip went a little more slowly.

It was almost one when they arrived at their destination. Bob's place was nice but wasn't designed for eight adults and three children. Mrs. Johnson shared a bed with Joey. Sam and Nancy shared a bed with Little Sammy. Bob, Terry, Lori, and Mary slept on cots or sofas. Kurt slept in the back room in a sleeping bag. No one complained.

After figuring out the sleeping arrangements, Bob wanted everyone to listen to a new record album he'd bought. He played the song "Grandma's Featherbed" by John Denver. They listened to it two or three times, and everyone laughed. It was a fun song. Then they listened to the rest of the album. The whole thing was perfect. Everyone enjoyed it.

Later that afternoon, something was needed from a nearby 7-Eleven. Kurt and Mary volunteered to get it. They were glad to get out for a while. It was a few blocks away, and they walked. This was a first for both of them. Neither had ever been to a convenience store. Back home, service stations sold gas and not much else. They might have a vending machine for sodas and candy bars, but that was it. Kurt and Mary were fascinated by it. It reminded them of a neighborhood grocery store that had been modernized.

When they got back, everyone was still sitting around talking. Bob suggested he run by McDonald's for dinner and bring food home for everyone. Kurt had never been to a McDonald's, so he didn't know what was available. Bob suggested a Big Mac, and Kurt agreed.

He'd never had such a large burger before. It was exotic in its time. After dinner, Kurt and Mary sat in the back room and listened to some music. Everyone loaded up in the cars around 7:30 and went downtown. Bob's office was high up in one of the tallest buildings in Indianapolis. He wanted to show it to everyone. Kurt was impressed by Bob's office. It had deep burgundy carpet with a dark walnut desk and furnishings. On the wall behind the desk was a parchment-colored print of an ancient world map from the sixteenth or seventeenth century. On either side of the wall hanging were tall sets of dark walnut bookcases. On the sidewalls were rows of filing cabinets, with various prints decorating the walls. It was very impressive. This office oozed success. Bob was very proud of it.

Then he had everyone turn around and look at the wall opposite the desk. It was filled with windows. They could see streets radiating from the city's center like spokes in a wheel. Bob explained the layout of Indianapolis. At the center of the city was the Circle, which went around the Veterans' Memorial. The streets that went off from there were set at angles. In the nighttime, streetlights and the headlights of the vehicles traveling up and down them defined the outline. It was a pretty view of a major city. Kurt had never seen anything like it.

After that, they headed back home. On the way, they drove around the Circle, passing the Indianapolis 500 Speedway and a few other points of interest. Then everyone unloaded and went inside.

Kurt was to sleep in a sleeping bag on the floor near the back door. He didn't care where he slept. He'd spent the entire day with Mary. It was his first visit to a major city other than St. Louis. There were lots of new things to see and experience. He settled on the floor to sleep after finding a moment alone with Mary where they whispered their good nights, embraced, and kissed. There seemed to be a thousand things racing through his mind, but he was also tired. He realized how much his body ached from the combination of the game the night before and the drive that morning. But soon enough, he fell into a deep sleep.

The following day was busy. Eleven people dressed and had

breakfast, all in a small two-bath condominium. Some of the families wanted larger breakfasts. People prepared eggs, sausage, bacon, and pancakes. Someone asked what Kurt wanted, and Mary laughingly answered for him. "He always has two slices of toast with peanut butter and a glass of Nestle's chocolate milk."

Everyone chuckled at this. Some of them looked at Kurt for confirmation. He nodded. They laughed even more. Someone said, "Well, at least there's one low-maintenance person here."

Kurt thought the idea of going to the circus was pretty cheesy. The only circuses he'd ever seen were those with only five or six members who played small towns. They would usually have one exotic animal. It was usually an elephant, but occasionally a lion, and one time a camel. He'd only gone to one or two of these as a little boy and had since avoided them.

They all loaded up and went downtown for the performance. The seats were excellent. Mary and Kurt had Joey parked by them. Joey was fascinated by all the animals. Anytime the elephants came out, he was on his feet. The lions and tigers intrigued him. The horses caught his attention as well. Joey was also enjoying the snacks Kurt and Mary got for him. He was having a wonderful day.

Kurt found himself enjoying the circus. Part of that can be attributed to his appreciation of how exciting it was for Joey. *I'd be excited by this if I was a little boy. This is nothing like the circuses I saw.* Kurt also enjoyed the trapeze artists and the acrobats. With three rings, it was impossible to take in everything that was happening. As they held hands watching the circus, Kurt and Mary exchanged glances and gently squeezed hands to let each other know they were both enjoying the show and enjoying one another.

After it was over, the group headed back to Bob's place. They all visited for around thirty minutes and then prepared to go home. The arrangements were the same as the trip to Indianapolis. They stopped around 6:00 p.m. for dinner, which was uneventful, and then on home. They pulled up in front of Kurt's house, where he said goodbye, got out of the car, and headed inside.

Mr. and Mrs. Kellerman were watching television when Kurt walked in. His mother saw him first. "Did you have a good time? What did you do?"

"It was fun. The circus was great. There were acrobats, trapeze artists, and just about every kind of animal you could imagine. We went to one of the tallest buildings in the city. You could see for miles from her brother's office. We drove by the Indianapolis 500 Speedway. Mary's family is nice."

"It sounds like you had a nice time, son. I'm glad you enjoyed it."

Kurt showered and got ready for bed. It took him a while to doze off as he rethought the things he'd seen and experienced over the weekend. Everyone seemed to have enjoyed the trip. Lori would argue with anyone if the talk turned to religion or politics, but that was just Lori. Spending a weekend with the Johnson family was more fun than it ever was with the Kellerman family.

Then Kurt's thoughts turned to Mary. He loved that she dozed off on his shoulder as they were on the long drive home. He could have sat there with his arm around her forever— watching her breathing, feeling her heart beating, one arm around her shoulder and the other hand holding her hand, staring at her face. Kurt fell asleep. It was almost as though Mary were still there with her head lying against him, sleeping, and then he joined her in that deep sleep.

Day by Day

After a busy weekend, things went back to normal. School each day, football practice after school, going home, having dinner, and calling Mary and talking on the phone. Friday night was always a football game. Saturday was Kurt coming over after lunch, spending time with Mary and attending Mass, catching a movie, and returning to Mary's. Sunday, Kurt went to church with his parents. He went to Mary's house in the afternoon and took her to his church on Sunday night.

There were a few variations from their established routine. The homecoming football game was on Saturday afternoon instead of Friday. Kurt took Mary to a movie on Friday night. After the game on Saturday, he got a haircut, cleaned out his car, and prepared for the homecoming dance. He had a new suit to wear for the occasion. In the past, he'd always taken the least expensive route when buying flowers for a girl. Kurt wanted Mary to have something a little more special. Despite his mother's objections, he chose a rosebud corsage for Mary rather than carnations.

Kurt arrived to pick up Mary and found her in a beautiful golden dress. It flattered her complexion, hair, and eyes perfectly. The red rosebuds set the outfit off very well. Kurt looked at Mary. *I can't believe she's dating me.* At the dance, they went in and found a table. Kurt had gone to the homecoming dance as a sophomore and a junior. Not much of a dancer, he had only bopped to the Queen's Dance with his partner in previous years. On the other hand, he hadn't gone on more than that one date with either of them. He'd gone more out of peer pressure and social obligation. It sounded like a terrible way to spend an evening as far as he was concerned. This time it was different. He knew that Mary loved to dance. As much as he worried about looking like an idiot, Kurt wanted to take Mary and see her enjoy herself.

Kurt mustered up his courage and danced. He realized it was not what she was used to. She loved to dance. After sitting out a few dances, Kurt realized he needed to ask her to dance again, even though it made him feel ill. But when he was there with Mary, he forgot all about everyone else and no longer cared what anyone thought. He had Mary in his arms, and she was smiling her smile. What more could anyone want?

When it was over, he took Mary home. When he walked her to the door, he told her how beautiful she was. Again, a lingering embrace. Several slow, gentle kisses, almost swaying together as though dancing, until they pulled apart. She went inside, and Kurt floated to his car. He drove home and again fell asleep thinking about the evening he'd spent with Mary.

School was going well enough. Kurt had straight A's, and Mary made the Honor Roll. Kurt didn't study much. He wasn't sure if Mary did; if she did, he had no idea when she found time.

Instead of growing tired of one another, the more Kurt and Mary were together, the greater their anticipation was to see each other again. Mary was the most important person in his life. Not only that, he cared about Joey and Mrs. Johnson. He thought of them as his family. He tried to think of ways to help them. But the center of it all was to be with Mary. He couldn't imagine life without her.

Kurt didn't know what Mary thought of him. He couldn't even understand why she wanted to go out with him. But he knew when she looked at him with those brown eyes, they were filled with love. Whether they held hands, kissed, or embraced, they seemed to please one another. They laughed at each other's jokes. Kurt and Mary cared about one another. The more time they spent together, the happier they were.

Another Trip

At halftime of an away game, Kurt's mother and Mary walked up to him and tried to get his attention. He walked over and asked what they wanted.

Mary said, "Would you like to take another trip to Indianapolis?"

"Sure, when are we leaving?"

His mother said, "At six tomorrow morning."

Kurt laughed. "I might sleep half the way there, but okay. I'll be ready."

When he got home from the game, he hurried and packed an overnight bag. No one had mentioned why they were making this trip. But Kurt didn't care. If he could spend the weekend with Mary, he would be overjoyed. He was torn between wondering what they would do and trying to get some sleep.

The next morning, he stumbled out of bed, dressed, and grabbed a quick breakfast, skipping the toast and only having the Nestle's Quik. Then he picked up his bag and sat in the living room, watching for the Johnsons to come by. They pulled up at five after six, and Kurt hurried out. He threw his bag in the trunk and crawled into the back seat with Mary. Everyone said hello, but they were all sleepy.

Kurt and Mary talked for a while, and then he dozed off. The next thing he knew, they pulled over to get gas and take a comfort stop. It was about half past eight. Kurt took Joey with him to the restroom. It felt good to get out of the car. He stretched his arms and legs. Joey bolted and ran toward the car. Kurt had to dash after him and grab his arm to stop him.

"Joey, you can't run out like that, or someone will run over you!"

"You're not the boss of me! I wasn't doing anything wrong! Let me go!"

Joey twisted away and tried to get loose, but Kurt's grip was too firm. Rather than accept defeat, Joey screamed and cried as loudly as possible. Kurt escorted Joey back to the car.

Mrs. Johnson wanted an explanation as to what was going on. Kurt explained what had happened and asked if he should have done anything differently. "No," said Mrs. Johnson, "if that is really what happened, you handled it fine."

Kurt felt there was some doubt in Mrs. Johnson's mind about what happened. Nancy had taken Little Sammy in and changed his diaper. She got in the car and said, "Thank heavens you were keeping an eye on Joey, Kurt. I was sure he was about to run in front of that car."

That resolved the issue. Mrs. Johnson thanked him too. Finally, everyone was back in the car. They powered through for a few more hours and reached Bob's home. Everyone was glad the drive was over. Kurt discovered Lori and Terry were arriving later in the day. After lunch, Sam, Nancy, and Little Sammy went with Bob somewhere. Mrs. Johnson walked into one of the guest bedrooms with a television and lay down. Kurt didn't know her problems, but one was a bad back. Sitting in the car for more than five hours was very painful for her. Mary and Kurt babysat Lisa and Joey.

Mary took the lead. She read stories and played some games with the children. Then she told them that Kurt was taking all of them for a walk. Kurt was surprised and mouthed, "What should I do?"

She took him aside. "Just walk anywhere. Point out anything you notice, and see if you can get them to ask questions. You can answer their questions. Or you can make up stories about what you see. Anything that makes it seem interesting to the kids." Kurt understood what was needed now. He took them on a walk. In no time, he had the children pretending a giant was chasing them. After several narrow escapes, they returned home, laughing and giggling.

Mary put Lisa down for a nap a little while later. Joey was

watching television. Kurt and Mary enjoyed the chance to talk. It was nice to have a little privacy. A little while later, Lori and Terry arrived. Bob, Sam, Nancy, and Little Sammy returned about thirty minutes later. Everyone was now at Bob's house.

The conversation was lively. Once again, Little Sammy wanted to toy with Kurt and snatch Kurt's glasses. The two of them were having a great time. Joey and Lisa played together. Lori sat down with Kurt and Little Sammy.

"I'm curious. You seem to like Little Sammy; how would you discipline him?"

Kurt stopped everything he was doing. "I have no idea. I suppose I'd tell him no. He's so little; I don't think you could do much more than that."

"I thought you probably thought it was okay to hit children to make them mind."

"I wouldn't call it hitting them. But if you mean spanking a child, I think if the child is old enough and you aren't angry when you do it, a few swift swats can work wonders."

"That's what conservatives always say to justify beating children."

"I would want anyone who beat a child to go to prison. There's a difference between beating and a few light swats on the fanny."

"What would you 'swat' them with? A belt or a razor strap?"

"Nothing like that. Mom and Dad used their hands. I guess that's what I'd do."

"What about twisting their arms? Would you do that?"

"Of course not."

"Well, you twisted Joey's arm today to punish him."

Kurt sighed. "No, I didn't. When Joey started to run in front of a car, I grabbed his arm to prevent him from getting run over. Ask Nancy. She saw the whole thing."

Lori glared at Kurt but didn't say anything. She went over and sat by Terry. Nancy was visiting with Mary. They hadn't heard the conversation with Lori. Nancy was enjoying herself. Mary saw Lori march off and looked questioningly at Kurt. "Later," he mouthed to her.

Bob, Sam, and Terry enjoyed remembering family activities from the past, including some of their favorite swimming holes and hiking trails. After dinner, the conversation bogged down a little. Lori was still staring at Kurt, frowning with her arms crossed. Everyone but Lori seemed to be having a great time.

After dinner, Lori presented a bizarre scenario in which she envisioned herself as the hero. Kurt butted in and said that although he was sure she would've been noble, her course of action probably wasn't the best. With a sharp elbow, Mary got Kurt to be quiet. *Lori is so much like my sister. She's a know-it-all, liberal wannabe hippie. Both of them get my goat.* He realized he should have kept his mouth shut, but it was too late. He steered clear of any other argumentative discussions the rest of the weekend.

Lori tried to provoke Kurt a few more times that evening. It was as though she was taunting him, hoping for a reaction. Kurt didn't take the bait. He smiled and refused to be drawn into another argument.

Things cooled off, and the conversation returned to more ordinary topics for the rest of the night. Mary and Kurt stayed up late talking. They couldn't seem to understand what this trip was about.

"I'm sorry I argued with Lori."

"It's not that important. But we do need to keep Mom and Lori happy about our relationship. I'm worried the argument cost us a little."

"I don't know if I'll ever learn to keep my mouth shut."

"I have my doubts about that." Mary laughed. "I'm not angry about it. I want them to like you."

"Well, I don't think Lori will ever like me. She accused me of punishing Joey by twisting his arm on the way here. Remember when I grabbed him to stop him from running in front of that car?"

"You're kidding!" Mary was furious. "No wonder you felt like arguing with her. But we still want to get on her good side."

The two of them listened to music; Mary got ready for bed. Kurt kissed her good night before he crawled into his sleeping bag.

The next day, they all took a driving tour of Indianapolis. Kurt and Mary rode with Lori and Terry. Mary nudged Kurt.

"I'd like to apologize for arguing with you last night."

"If you're going to spend time with me, you better know how to argue."

Terry looked at Lori. "She's got that right."

"I still think you were wrong, Kurt."

"I never doubted that for a minute. Neither one of us changes his mind easily."

"Or HER mind."

"Don't let her kid you; Lori likes nothing better than a good argument. I think you and Bob are the only two members of this family who aren't afraid of her."

"Terry, he's not a member of this family yet."

Mary joined in the conversation and asked Terry something about his work. The two of them successfully changed the subject and avoided an uncomfortable discussion. The rest of the group returned later than Lori, Terry, Mary, and Kurt.

When everyone did get home, they ordered pizza delivery for dinner. Kurt wondered when they were going to head back home. While they ate, someone mentioned that *The Last Picture Show* would be on television that night. It was unanimous that everyone wanted to watch it. Kurt wasn't the least bit inter-ested, but his attitude was that whatever everyone else wanted to do was okay with him. This meant they would not get home until four or five in the morning.

Kurt sat on the end of the sofa with Mary to his right,

leaning against him. He placed his arm around her. She grasped his left hand with hers. Everyone started watching the movie. Bob was lying on the floor with a pillow under his head. Not too far into the movie, Little Sammy crawled up to Bob, sat upright, and started rubbing and patting Bob's bald spot.

It was one of those things that made everyone laugh, even Bob. When the movie was over, they loaded up and headed for home. It was around midnight when they left. Joey and Little Sammy fell asleep. Everyone else talked in low voices, but not about anything important. Kurt had called ahead and explained to his parents it would be early morning before he got home. As they drove along, he alternated between looking at Mary's face and out the window at the stars. Mary leaned up against Kurt and dozed off.

Eventually, Kurt nodded off as well. They did have two comfort stops and bought gasoline. The road they chose to come home on was different from the one they had taken before. It had lots of potholes and bumps. The ride was rough, and Sam drove more slowly than usual. The constant thump, thump, thump of the tires against the road awakened Kurt and Mary. At each thump, there was bone-jarring bouncing throughout the vehicle. After a long drive, they got home. Kurt thanked them for inviting him on the trip and said goodbye. He went into his house and collapsed on his bed.

His alarm went off two hours later, and he stumbled to breakfast. His mother told him to go back to bed. She would awaken him so he could go to school after lunch. With no argument, he thanked her and stumbled back to bed, where he collapsed and fell asleep.

Mary didn't show up at school that day. Kurt called as soon as football practice was over. Everything was okay. Mary told Kurt that she, her mother, and Joey were exhausted and needed to sleep. Kurt told her that was what he assumed, but he wanted to check.

What??

When Kurt talked to Mary at school on Tuesday morning, she looked worried. "What's wrong, Mary? Is there a problem?"

"I don't know, but I'm worried. Sam and Nancy are coming over tonight. They want to talk over some plans with Mom and me. There was something about it that scared me. I asked if you could be there, and they said yes. Will you come? Please?"

"Of course I will. What time do I need to be there? Are you sure you don't know what it's about?"

"It might be about something I know about, and it's so awful that I don't want to say. I pray that I'm wrong. But I don't think I can deal with this if I don't have you with me. Can you be at our house by seven?"

"Absolutely! I will be there. If it needs to be earlier, let me know. Surely it isn't as bad as you're thinking. Everything will be all right. But I'll be there with you and for you."

Kurt put his arms around her. All through the rest of the day, it seemed as though a cloud was hanging over them. Kurt's mind wandered all afternoon. He couldn't imagine what was happening or what Mary thought might be happening. Still, it couldn't be that bad.

After football practice, Kurt went home for dinner and then went to Mary's house. Sam and Nancy were already there. He knocked on the door, and Mary opened it. It looked like she'd been crying. He started to ask what was wrong, but she raised a finger to his lips. He went on in and sat by her on the sofa.

Then Sam proceeded to tell a story. His store had been audited a month ago. There were some irregularities in the books. The two men spent two days going through them and accused Sam of stealing thousands of dollars from the business. None of this was true, but they got in his face. They were threatening him with jail and bankruptcy. If he did not sign a confession they had prepared, they would press charges, and he would be in prison before the end of the year. If he signed the papers, he would lose the franchise and his job but have no further financial liability. Sam was terrified and signed the papers, even though he claimed they were filled with lies.

Sam had talked to Bob and his attorney about this. Both said he shouldn't have signed the paper, but it was too late. He was finished in the town he now lived in and was going to relocate to Indianapolis. Bob had helped him find a place to live over the weekend. Also, because no one else lived close to Mrs. Johnson, Mary, and Joey, they would move in with Bob, who was searching for a house in Indianapolis that would hold all of them.

He can't be serious. Why should Mary, Joey, and Mrs. Johnson move just because Sam's an idiot? There's got to be something else we can do. I won't let them take Mary away. They've already stolen her childhood. They can't do this to her.

Kurt asked, "When is everyone planning on moving?" He felt like he was in a dream. This couldn't be real. It couldn't be happening.

"We will all be moving on Thanksgiving Day next month," Sam answered.

Kurt looked at Mary. The tears flowed down her cheeks now. Kurt tried to fight his tears, although he could feel his eyes were about to flood. He hugged Mary and held on to her tight.

"We'll make it through this," he whispered.

Turning to Sam and Mrs. Johnson, Kurt asked, "Could Mary move in with my family and finish her schooling here? She would be more than welcome. My parents like her. Our house is big enough she could have her own bedroom and bath if that would make a difference."

A quick answer came back. "No. She needs to live with Mom so that they can all get their social security survivor benefits from Dad."

"We aren't interested in receiving any money. She could live with us rent-free. We'd take care of her."

"No, we all need to be together during this," Sam responded.

There it was. Mary was moving more than five hours away in one month. There was nothing Kurt and Mary could do about it. They both sat there in a state of shock. Kurt tried to be strong for Mary, but his heart pounded. His eyes filled with tears that had not yet leaked out. He needed to blow his nose. He slipped off to the restroom, washed his face, and blew his nose. Then he came back to his seat. As he sat down, Kurt gave Mary a weak smile. He tried to be bright and optimistic. Sam and his family left.

Mary and Kurt pledged to do everything they could to make this work. When Kurt left, they embraced, kissed, and held one another. He had a tissue to wipe the tears from her eyes. They kissed good night, and he left after she went back inside.

That night, he did not run or float to the car. Going to the car seemed more like a death march. It felt as though the drive home took forever instead of five minutes. He went up to bed. But there was no sleep. Kurt thought of a million ways for Mary not to move, but he knew her family would not accept them. He would have to learn to date a girl who lived five or six hours away. It wasn't going to be easy, but they could do it.

The following week was a roller coaster for them. At times, they were as happy as ever. Then something would remind them of the impending move, making it difficult to function.

Kurt asked his parents if he could talk to them. "Mary has to move to Indianapolis. Would you consider letting her live here?"

Mrs. Kellerman spoke first. "Why does she have to move?"

"One of Mary's brothers has financial problems and needs to move away. He takes care of a lot of things around the house for them. Her brothers have talked it over and think her mom should move in with her older brother Bob and that Mary and her little brother need to move too."

Mr. Kellerman said, "If they've decided, we shouldn't interfere. We should respect their decision." He exchanged a wary glance with Kurt's mother.

"But they aren't considering Mary's feelings. We have three spare bedrooms. She's a good housekeeper and a good cook. You know how nice she is. She wouldn't be any trouble. You allowed a second or third cousin to live here three years ago."

Mr. Kellerman glanced at his wife. She nodded without looking. Kurt realized they were trying to bring an end to this without having to say no. "But he was on your mother's side of the family. Besides, he was a boy."

"As far as I'm concerned, Mary is family. And yes, she's a girl, but I promise that nothing inappropriate would go on. You can trust us both on that."

"Son, there's no point in discussing this. She's a fine girl, but we should let her family decide. It's none of our business."

"Dad, it's my business. Mary thinks of you like you're her parents. She goes to church with us. She goes to ball games with you. She spends more time with you than any of your children but me. Can I at least ask the Johnsons to consider it? Won't you agree to it if they decide it's what's best for Mary?"

"I think you just need to be quiet and let them take care of it as best they can. I think we've talked about this enough."

They don't care. Never mind their future daughter-in-law's heart is broken. That mine is broken. They aren't going to help.

"If I can persuade the Johnsons, would you let Mary stay here? That's all I'm asking."

"They're never going to agree to it. That's the end of the conversation."

His father got up and left the room, followed by Mrs. Kellerman. Kurt stood there, lost in his thoughts. He'd been confident his parents would come to the rescue.

He kept trying to find something that would work, but he also wanted to make each day as normal as possible. He did his best to spend as much time with Mary as possible or talk to her on the phone. She consumed his thoughts. She was holding up well. Kurt determined he would be everything he could be for her.

On Thursday, during a game of soccer in PE, someone kicked Kurt and split his big toe on the right foot open. It had been broken years before when he was in junior high. Kurt went to the doctor and got his toe stitched up. The doctor told him no strenuous use of the toe and no soccer. He told the doctor he had a football game on Friday night.

The doctor said, "You can't play tomorrow night. The stitches could break, and you might injure the toe even more."

Kurt pleaded with the doctor. "I haven't missed a game in four seasons. Please let me play my final two games."

"Here's what we're going to do. We will bandage that toe as much as possible and give you some pain relievers. You can only take them twice. One hour before the game and six hours later if you still need it. I will bandage this so it can't get hurt."

Kurt took the pills in the locker room before going out on the field and was ready for action. Things were going well. His toe wasn't bothering him at all. He played center, and the other team kept blitzing the middle linebacker. Kurt and the quarterback agreed that when this happened, they would run a quarterback sneak to whichever side the linebacker was not coming from. Kurt could block the nose tackle into the linebacker, and they gained large chunks of yards in each play. Finally, in one play, the linebacker faked a blitz. They drove forward for around seven yards, but more and more players from the other team were piling on. Eventually, it became too much, and the pile collapsed.

Unfortunately, Kurt's right foot was caught and couldn't move with him. It ended up pressed flat against his leg. There was an immediate hot, burning sensation. *This can't be good.* When he got up from the pile, his right ankle did not work. He limped off the field, shouting that they needed a sub at center. The trainer went to work taping up his right foot. By the time he was finished, Kurt felt no pain and wanted to return to the game.

The coach sent him in. He could still block effectively, and once again, they were gaining five-to-ten-yard chunks running up the middle. But it was also clear that something was wrong with Kurt's ankle. When he walked, he had to throw his right leg forward. He wasn't walking on it. The tape supported the ankle and kept it stable, but it had no strength. Kurt was called to the sideline.

"You're out of the game, Kellerman. Something's wrong with that ankle. Go sit on the bench and follow the trainer's instructions."

The trainer had him sit on a bench with his leg elevated and ice packs taped around his ankle. He spent the rest of the game that way. When Mary saw that he was out of the game for good, she came down and talked to him for the rest of the game.

When he got home that night, Kurt was in a lot of pain. He'd forgotten about the pain medicine and had a miserable night. On Saturday morning, his mother took him to the doctor. He had a nasty high ankle sprain. The doctor taped it up and put him on crutches for the next week. His football career was over. Kurt wasn't happy, but there was nothing he could do. He hobbled around on crutches until Friday night.

On Monday, Kurt had his stitches removed at a follow-up visit with his doctor. He missed part of the school day. Mary came by after school with his homework assignments. They sat and talked for an hour before she went home. It was the best hour of the day as far as Kurt was concerned.

One of Kurt's best friends, Roger Sloan, had a knee injury at football practice. He was on crutches along with Kurt, waiting to have surgery. They ran around together after school, as neither needed to go to practice anymore. They went to the record store on Monday, and Kurt bought a new album he thought Mary would like, *Wrap Around Joy* by Carole King. Kurt took it over to Mary's and left it with her.

Roger didn't have a girlfriend, so Mary kept offering to fix him up. She liked to tease him. But with every girl she suggested, he responded with a no. There was nothing wrong with the girls, but Roger already had someone in mind. He must have been spot-on because he eventually married that girl. Still, teasing Roger provided a little relief to the turmoil that Kurt and Mary were both feeling.

Chapter 6
November 1974

Playing for Time

Mary's mother went into the hospital on the last day of October. She and Kurt visited her mother every evening. Part of the time, Joey came with them, but he went to stay with Uncle Sam and Aunt Nancy in November.

On the first day of November, Kurt went back to the doctor. They cut off most of the tape on his ankle. It was thick, almost like a cast. He was off crutches at this point too. When he got home, he went to pick up Mary. They visited her mother at the hospital and then went to the final football game of the year. Kurt was unused to walking, and his legs were a little tired. Mary had lots of questions about moving, so they left the game early to have some peace.

Alone together, they fell into one another's arms. This was their first time truly alone in quite some time. They listened to some of their favorite albums and lay on the sofa, holding one another as tightly as possible. Things continued this way as long as Mrs. Johnson was in the hospital. Finally, she came home after around two weeks.

Kurt and Mary needed to run an errand to Sam and Nancy's one day. Sam's home was around twenty miles away. Kurt stopped to introduce Mary to one of his favorite aunts. They visited for about thirty minutes and then went to finish their errand. When they got back home, Kurt spent the rest of the evening with Mary. They no longer wanted to go to movies and such. They just wanted to talk and hold one another. Each moment was precious and more valuable than gold.

All their ideas for allowing Mary to remain in town had been rejected. They hadn't even been listened to by the Johnsons. As far as her family was concerned, Mary was moving to Indianapolis, and that was that. The decision had been made long before, and Mary's feelings and thoughts did not matter. Some members of her family recognized her pain but still felt it was the right thing to do.

One Tuesday night, Kurt needed a favor from Mary. In his creative writing class, he was supposed to submit his short story for the semester typewritten. Kurt was not a good typist. He made mistake after mistake. Mary excelled at typing. She agreed to take care of it. He brought his manuscript over after dinner. The short story was 3,500 words. The class limits were a minimum of 3,000 words and a maximum of 6,000.

Mary dove in and started typing. She had to stop numerous times to determine what Kurt had written. He had horrible handwriting, and she sometimes had to ask him questions. At other points, she wanted to make sure of the punctuation and other issues. It took her a little over two hours to complete it. Then she and Kurt did a quick proofread to ensure they hadn't missed anything. Finally, they were done. It was nearly ten o'clock.

Kurt opened the door to leave and laid the manuscript on a table. He took Mary into his arms, thanked her, and kissed her long. She kissed him back, and they went on for a few minutes. A car drove by, and Kurt stiffened. His father had just gone by and seen them standing in the doorway. Kurt was furious. His entire body was trembling. His face burned. He kissed Mary good night one last time, grabbed his short story, and headed home.

When he got in the house, he said, "Dad, what's going on? Why were you driving by Mary's house a few minutes ago? You knew where I was and what I was doing there."

"I knew you were there. But that didn't look much like schoolwork to me. You should be home at ten o'clock on a school night."

"Dad, I told you she was typing a 3,500-word short story from my handwriting and that it would take most of the evening. What you saw was me thanking her and saying good night!" Kurt was letting his temper show. His body was shaking. His voice quivered. His fists were clenched. Kurt was ready to blow up.

"You weren't thanking her, and you weren't saying good night. You were smooching!" His father was now letting out his temper. Mr. Kellerman's voice was raised. He'd dropped his newspaper and was staring at his son with fire in his eyes.

"We weren't doing anything wrong. I thought you trusted me. I thought you knew Mary. I'm going to my room." Kurt left the room. It was hours before he got to sleep that night. He was upset with his father. He was angry. Hurt. Somehow, he felt his father had betrayed him.

The Final Week

On Mary's final weekend in town, Kurt went to Mass with her on Saturday night one last time. She went with him to his church on Sunday night for the final time. They saw one another every day, first at school and then after.

On Monday, they had a double date with one of Mary's best friends, Patty, and her boyfriend, Steve. They went to get pizza and just hung out and talked for an hour after eating. It was nice of Patty to want to say goodbye to Mary. *I appreciate it, but I wish I could spend more time with Mary alone.*

Tuesday night, Kurt took Mary to one of the nicer restaurants in the area. It was about thirty miles away. Mary was sitting tightly at Kurt's side as he drove along. His right arm was around her shoulder, holding her close. They listened to some of their favorite music as they went down the road. There was some conversation, but it was hard to know what to say. In forty-eight hours, Mary would be in Indianapolis. Landline phone calls that far away were expensive. It felt like their world was being crushed all around them.

At the restaurant, Mary ordered a salad and some pasta with meatballs. Kurt asked for a salad, steak, and baked potato. Neither of them wanted dessert. They talked more in the restaurant than they had on the road. They had so much they wanted to say but had already said so many times. It was hard to say goodbye to someone you loved.

On the drive home, they were again as close as they could be in Kurt's car. He stole glances at her face as often as he could. Sometimes she seemed to be looking far away with sadness. Now and then, she looked up at him with her special smile and piercing brown eyes. *She's the most beautiful person, the sweetest and kindest person I've ever known.*

On one of those occasions, as his eyes were drinking in her beauty and his thoughts were on all her wonderful attributes, Kurt noticed out of the corner of his eye that something was wrong. They were going around a nearly ninety-degree turn, and he wasn't turning or slowing down. He let up on the accelerator, hit the brakes, and turned into the curve. Mary jumped.

"What happened?" she said.

"I was so busy watching you that I forgot to watch the road. You have the most beautiful brown eyes, the prettiest smile, and the sweetest face in the world. I'll never forget this moment if I live to be one hundred."

They drove on in silence for a few minutes. Kurt was still looking at her, and she was still watching him. They both smiled. Even though a great deal of pain was coming, they were happy at that moment. They were blessed. And they knew it.

The night before Thanksgiving, Kurt's brother and sister (and their spouses) were in town. He did something he'd never done before in his life. He brought a girl home to meet all of them. Kurt warned her they were not always nice and could be stuck-up. But she wanted to meet his family.

Kurt picked Mary up and brought her back to his house. He opened the door and showed her into the living room." Mary, you already know Mom and Dad. This is my brother, Edward, and his wife Elizabeth. They live in Jefferson City, Missouri. Edward, Elizabeth, this is Mary Johnson."

They both nodded to Mary and said, "Hello."

"Hello. It's nice to meet you."

Kurt turned to the other couple. "This is my sister, Judy, and her husband, Jerry Reilly. They live in Yorkville, Illinois. Judy, Jerry, this is Mary."

They both said, "Hello, Mary."

"Hello. I'm happy to meet you."

Kurt and Mary sat on the sofa. *They weren't very friendly to Mary. This could be an awful last night together. I should have taken Mary out again so we could be alone.* But Kurt was wrong. For once in his life, Kurt's family was laughing and joking. Edward started telling some stories from his teens that made everyone laugh.

Kurt's mom had prepared a nice dinner, and everyone enjoyed it. They made Mary feel welcome. It went better than Kurt could have ever imagined. Kurt and Mary left after spending a couple of hours with his family.

"Do you want to go back to your house?"

"No, they're already loading up the U-Haul truck. I don't want to go there until I have to."

"What about tomorrow? Mom's extended family all come to our house. You're welcome to come too."

Mary looked away. "Thank you. I wish I could. But I have to help load the moving truck tomorrow morning."

"I can come and help. At least we could spend the morning together."

There was a long pause. "No, I don't want you to help them move me away. I don't want to move away. If you help, somehow it would be like you were approving it. Please come by at half past twelve. We aren't leaving until one. That will give us thirty minutes or so to say goodbye. I don't think I could stand any longer than that. I'm not sure I can stand that."

Tears were streaming down her cheeks. Kurt pulled into a vacant parking lot. He wrapped her up in his arms.

"I love you more than I ever thought it was possible to love someone. I don't know how to say goodbye to you. I can't. But I will be there for you. I thank God that you are a part of my life. I'm just waiting for the day when we can be together and no one can separate us."

After several long kisses, Mary said, "I feel the same way. I don't know how I can make this move without you. I love you so much. You're the best thing that ever happened to me. I'll write to you as soon as I know my new address and have something to write with. I'll give you my phone number as soon as possible."

Goodbye

Kurt spent a sleepless night. He got up in the morning. Afterward, the extended family started arriving. They had big football games on Thanksgiving Day. One before dinner and another after. For the first time in years, Kurt didn't play. He just wandered around the house and yard. Dinner was a little late. They usually ate at noon. This year, it was about 12:15 when Thanksgiving dinner was served. Kurt didn't care. He couldn't eat anyway. He slipped out, got in his car, and drove to Mary's.

They were loading the last few things on the U-Haul as he pulled in and parked. They were having sandwiches for lunch. Mary wasn't eating anything either. Kurt and Mary went for a short walk hand-in-hand. After a little while, they heard a horn honking. They returned to her house and were told it was time to get in the car and go. One last time, they held each other tight and kissed goodbye. Tears streamed down both their cheeks. There was nothing more to say. It was happening, and they could do nothing to stop it.

But they knew their love would prevail, no matter what. This was their life. And that life would be the two of them together. Anything else was unthinkable. Kurt stood watching as the caravan of cars pulled away. She was gone. Gone. He drove around for a couple of hours before going home. The extended family was still there. He couldn't stand it. He felt like he was suffocating. Finally, they began to leave.

As soon as the last one left, Kurt's mom walked up. "Where did you disappear to?"

"I went to say goodbye to Mary."

"It doesn't take that long to say goodbye to someone. We had a house full of company here, and you walked out on them."

Kurt looked at her like he'd never seen her before. "Mom, don't push me on this. Today was the worst day of my life. I had to say goodbye to Mary and compose myself before I came home."

"I think the two of you are just a little too serious for high school kids."

Kurt walked off without saying anything else. He'd never seen this side of his mother in his life. It was not something he ever wanted to witness again. She'd managed to take a terrible day and somehow make it even more painful. He left the house again so that he could be alone. He couldn't stand any more conversation that day.

That night, Kurt asked himself how far Mary and her family had gone. He wondered just where she was. He went to bed, wondering how long it would take to hear something from her. At this point, she didn't even have an address or a phone number. All he could do was wait. And while he waited, all he could think about was how much he already missed her. Kurt didn't think he could ever have a day worse than November 28.

He spent the rest of Thanksgiving with his family. After Thanksgiving Day, Kurt's brother, Edward, spent most of his time with Elizabeth's family. Her mother, uncle, and some cousins still lived in their hometown. Judy and Jerry visited some friends but stayed until Sunday morning. At lunch on Saturday, Judy announced they would be leaving on Sunday morning around nine; Kurt's mother got angry.

"You're not coming to church and staying for Sunday dinner? Why not?"

"Mom, we've got a six-hour drive to get home. Traffic is going to be heavy. If we leave at nine, we can get home before dark."

Mr. Kellerman said, "It wouldn't hurt you and Jerry to attend church for once."

"Dad, I don't need to hear that right now. We want to get home and rest before we go to work tomorrow. That's it."

Thank heavens they didn't blow up like this on Wednesday night. This is the garbage I expect when my family gets together. The rest of the afternoon was strained. Judy called an old high school friend and went with her for a girls' night out. Jerry hung out with Kurt. Mr. and Mrs. Kellerman sulked through dinner. Jerry took Kurt for a drive. They stopped at Dairy Queen and both had hot fudge sundaes with marshmallow cream and nuts. It was Jerry's favorite.

"You seem kind of down this weekend, Kurt. It wasn't that fight between your sister and your folks, was it?"

"No. Mary moved to Indianapolis on Thursday. I'm struggling to cope with it."

"The girl you brought over Wednesday night? Why did she move?"

"It's a long story. There wasn't anything either one of us could do about it. Mom got mad because I left the house on Thanksgiving Day to go and tell her goodbye. The last three days have been rough."

"I'm sorry. I didn't know. I'm glad I have you to hang out with tonight. I get frustrated with Judy bringing me down here and always leaving me alone. I worried that if I stayed at the house, they would pressure me to make Judy attend church on Sunday."

"They probably would. I'm glad you offered to take me out tonight. I've been sitting around missing Mary since she drove off. I wondered if Judy going out with her old friends all the time bothered you. I'm sorry. But I'm glad we're hanging out tonight."

"Between her making your parents mad about church and making me angry about being left alone while she hangs out with her friends, I dread coming here anymore. She usually blames me when we don't go to church with your folks. She tells them it's because I'm Catholic. You know, I haven't gone to church since I started high school. Judy doesn't have any interest in church. But she always uses me as the bad guy to keep your parents off her back."

Kurt had learned a lot that night. He felt bad for Jerry. It seemed like he was almost as miserable as Kurt.

Sunday at lunch, Kurt got to listen to his parents criticize Jerry. "That Jerry, the only reason Judy doesn't attend church is because he's a Catholic. If she hadn't married Jerry, they would be here right now. I cooked enough to feed us all, and now there are only three of us."

"You know, Mom, I discussed it with Jerry last night. He isn't interested in church. He wouldn't object, but Judy doesn't want to go. She blames Jerry, but he'd come with her if she wanted to attend."

"You don't know how Catholics are, son. I see them in the hardware store all the time. They get their children to marry non-Catholics and convert them. I know people who had to sign papers promising their children would be raised Catholic."

"Dad, Judy got married at our church. She didn't have to sign any papers. You know her politics and how wild she and her friends were in high school. She hasn't been interested in church for nearly ten years. She went while she lived at home, and the moment she left home, she quit."

"You just need to keep quiet. You don't understand these things."

Kurt quit talking. He used to have a good relationship with his parents, but over the last few months, that relationship had been stretched to the limit. He went to bed early. Lying there, he prayed for Mary and her family. It took him a while to fall asleep.

Chapter 7
December 1974

Waiting

School went on as usual for Kurt. He still had his friends, which only made him feel guilty. *Mary did not have her friends with her in the new place.* She was alone in a large city, in a large school.

Waiting to hear from her was painful. Kurt had no desire to be patient. Each day he hoped for a phone call or a letter.

Kurt didn't know what to do with all the free time he now possessed. Part of the time, he cruised town with his friends. They also got together one or two nights a week to play cards. On weekends, he watched sporting events on television. Nothing interested him.

In November, Kurt had sent off some college applications. His three primary efforts were directed at the University of Illinois, Indiana University, and Illinois State University. He applied to them after the bad news in October. They were all significantly closer to Indianapolis than home was. He was also thinking of Indiana State at Terre Haute. Until Mary left town, he hadn't thought about them that much. Now, he waited every day for some news.

He felt lost without Mary. It was not just that he didn't see her at school or on weekends. Never talking to her on the telephone or hearing anything about her was unbearable. *I wonder what she's doing.* Also, they were both in tears the last time they'd seen one another. He wondered how she coped with her new school, home, and life. Not knowing these things was as painful as not being with or talking to her.

For Kurt, it felt as though his life had been put on hold. He went through a routine like his life before he started dating Mary, but there was a vast void. He went through it with no sense of purpose. The only things he had any sense of anticipation about were the mail or the ringing of the telephone. But time after time, there was nothing from Mary. Neither was it ever Mary on the phone, although he ran to answer anytime he was home when it rang.

This went on for more than a week. Kurt felt discouraged. His friends tried to cheer him up, but he was inconsolable. He was obsessed with getting some word. There was a feeling of helplessness that he hated through all of this. At the same time, Kurt was worried about whether anything terrible had happened. Was Mary safe? Was she all right? What was going on with her and her family? He cursed Sam for doing this to Mary (and the rest of the family). The whole thing seemed bizarre, but there was nothing to be done but wait.

News

On Saturday, December 7, a letter from Mary was in the mail. The envelope was light yellow, with Mary's handwriting on it. Kurt opened it and read it. There were two sheets of yellow paper with flowers on the corner borders. The handwriting was neat and pretty, like Mary's.

Dear Kurt,

Everything is going well. We spent Thanksgiving night at Bob's condominium. He signed the papers on the house the next day. It took most of Friday and Saturday to unload the U-Haul and unpack. As soon as we were finished unloading here, we went to Sam's new home and unloaded there.

Bob's new house is nice. It has a fireplace and is about a mile from my new school. There is already snow on the ground here. It took until Monday for us to finish unpacking. Joey likes that he has a larger bedroom and plays with Lisa daily. Everyone has separate bedrooms, which is nice.

My first day at school was Tuesday. Bob went with me. First, we took Joey to his school just a few blocks from mine. After we got him situated, Bob went into the high school with me. It's huge. I was nervous. I wish you were here with me. Bob took care of everything. He came with me and the vice principal to show me around to all of my classes. I had to get a parking permit to use the school's parking lot. That seemed strange. Everyone here has a reserved parking space. So far, it hasn't been terrible. I guess it will just take time. My history teacher reminds me of you. He likes history, like you, and is a football coach.

Bob has been trying to show me around our neighborhood and parts of the city. He warned me to avoid certain areas, as they aren't safe. He took me by a place so I could get some stationery and write to you after school today.

Sam, Nancy, and Little Sammy rent an apartment near here. I think we'll be seeing them a lot. Sam has a job. I think Bob got it for him.

I love and miss you more than I can ever say. You're always on my mind. I am putting our phone number and address at the bottom of the page. I can't wait to hear back from you. Please write or call as soon as you can.

With all my love,
Mary

Kurt read the letter three times. Then he took it and carefully put it away in the chest of his bedroom. He was overjoyed to hear from her. Kurt got a pen and paper and wrote to Mary, letting her know he'd received her letter.

Dear Mary,

I can't tell you how thrilled I was to receive your letter. I know it's only been nine days, but they were the longest nine days of my life. It sounds like you've been busy. Bob will take good care of you. After you, he's my favorite person in your family. It was nice of him to go with you to get registered at school and show you around. Be careful driving around Indianapolis. I'm glad he's showing you around.

I'm going to call you next Thursday night at seven. That should give you plenty of time to get this. Your letter only took two days to arrive. I can't wait to hear your voice. I miss you so much.

There isn't anything going on around here. I go to school, but I don't worry about getting there till the bell rings. I'm glad you like your history teacher. He sounds a lot better than Mr. Hall. I swear he's the most boring teacher I've ever known. After school, I go home and hang around the house. I did get out of the house for the first home basketball game to play in the pep band. It doesn't look like we'll have a good team this year.

By the way, I think your stationery is pretty. It seems perfect for you. When I saw the envelope, I thought it was from Mary. I'm the happiest I've been since the night before Thanksgiving. Who would think a letter could make me so happy? I hope this letter brings you some happiness. I love you with all my heart. You are the sweetest, kindest, most beautiful person I've ever known.

With all my love,
Kurt

Unfortunately for Mary, Kurt's handwriting was uneven and sloppy. He put every possible effort into being as neat as he could. Then he hurriedly addressed an envelope, put a stamp on it, and ran it to the post office, so she would receive it as soon as possible.

Mary wrote Kurt at least two or three times each week, and he wrote the same to her. He couldn't wait to find out if he had any mail. He was always on the lookout for yellow envelopes with her charming handwriting. They refreshed his soul. It made him think of one play his sophomore year when he'd extended as much as possible to catch a pass during a football game. Someone from the other team speared him in the chest with their helmet. It knocked the wind out of him. There was a panicky feeling for a moment as he breathed in and didn't receive any air. But while he lay there waiting, in a minute, as he breathed in, a refreshing wave of air rushed in to fill his lungs. That refreshing wave of air was what Mary's letters were to Kurt's soul.

Kurt received another important letter on Saturday, December 14. It was from the University of Illinois. He'd not only been accepted there but also received some scholarships. While he'd received acceptance letters from some other schools, none of them were offering the same scholarships. Kurt finished the paperwork accepting the scholarships. Then he started filling out the enrollment papers for the University of Illinois. He wrote a letter to Mary letting her know the news. Instead of being 225 miles away from her, by late August he would only be 115 miles away. It would cut the distance in half. Kurt was excited by this.

When Mary wrote back, she invited Kurt to come and visit during the Christmas holidays. He discussed it with his parents at dinner. "Mom, Dad, Mary has asked me to go and stay with her family for a few days over Christmas. May I please see her?"

"Kurt, we want you to be here when your brother and sister come for Christmas. It's a time for family."

She's going to get angry if I'm not careful. "Mom, Edward and Judy are getting here two days before Christmas. They're spending Christmas Day with us. Then they're all leaving on the morning after Christmas. I want to be here too. I want the whole family to be together for Christmas. I want to leave after they leave. Then I can spend a few days celebrating Christmas with Mary and her family."

"You will be here for Christmas Eve and Christmas Day?"

"Yes, ma'am."

"When will you get back home?"

"I was hoping to drive home on Sunday. I will leave Mary's house after lunch and get here for dinner. How does that sound, Dad?"

"Let me get this straight. Do you want to be gone for four whole days? That's a long time."

"Two of those days will be mainly driving. On the twenty-sixth, I won't get there until time for dinner on Thursday, then have Friday and Saturday together with Mary, and be home for dinner on Sunday the twenty-ninth. This means a lot to me."

His parents looked at one another. Finally, Kurt's father said, "Yes. You have our permission.

"Thank you, Dad. I appreciate it. You, too, Mom."

I'm going to see Mary. I can talk to her, kiss her, look at her, hold her hand. This is the best Christmas ever.

Mary was thrilled when she found that Kurt had called. She checked with her mother and got permission for Kurt to visit. The rest of the family would be there on Christmas Day but were also staying until Sunday. He started counting off the days. He'd called her on Thursday the nineteenth. His visit was only a week away.

Kurt's brother and sister arrived in town two days before Christmas. While they ate dinner, Mr. Kellerman made an announcement.

"There is a Christmas Eve service at church at 6:00 p.m. I hope you will all come."

Kurt saw Judy roll her eyes. Edward looked at Elizabeth with a question on his face. Jerry was busy eating and not paying much attention to the conversation.

"We're spending Christmas Eve with Elizabeth's family. We won't be able to go, Dad. Sorry about that. Maybe if we'd known earlier, but we've got everything planned."

"And I've promised to get together with my friend Joyce and her husband on Christmas Eve. Jerry and I can't go to church with you either."

Kurt remained silent but watched everyone. It was clear that Jerry had no idea they had plans for Christmas Eve. Edward waited until he got a signal from Elizabeth before answering. It was pretty clear that both of them could have attended the worship service. They both came up with quick excuses based on nonexistent previous commitments.

I wonder why Mom and Dad don't get it that none of the four of them want to go to church. It's so obvious. It's certainly not because Jerry was raised Catholic.

His parents didn't talk much for the rest of the meal. After a few minutes of silence, Kurt told Jerry about his plans to go to U of I. Then the rest of them joined in the conversation. Everyone was tired from the drive, so they went to bed early.

Christmas Eve, Kurt went to church in his car. He sat with a few friends. His parents were glad he was there but were upset their other children didn't come. It was a long night after they got back home. Christmas Day was uneventful. The men all watched a football game that afternoon. Kurt didn't know what the women did after lunch.

That night, Kurt wrapped the necklace he'd bought Mary for Christmas. He packed his bags, trying to anticipate what they would do while he was there. There were a few things he checked on his car. His Ford was not the best cold-weather car. He couldn't wait for Christmas Day to pass. On the day after

Christmas, he couldn't wait to get started. He and his brother left at the same time.

The speed limit of fifty-five miles per hour had been enforced since the oil embargo of 1973 caused the speed limit to be reduced nationwide. Around noon, he pulled in at a McDonald's and got a Big Mac. Then he continued north. There was no snow on the ground for two-thirds of his journey. He stopped to get gas before getting on I-70. After he crossed the state line and went through Terre Haute, he began to see patches of snow on the ground. The closer to Indianapolis he got, the more snow he saw. But the good news was the roads were clear. Mary had mailed detailed instructions on how to get to the house when he reached the city. They were laid out on the seat beside him.

As he approached the city, he went by the airport. He knew his interchange was just past there. He headed north, carefully watching for the right exit. There were no problems, as the directions were clear and brought him to the house. Cars were filling the driveway, so he parked on the street in front of the house. He was happy for the vehicles in the drive as he recognized one of them as Sam's and another as Terry's. He got out and headed toward the door. Before he even got to the door, Mary had thrown it open. She ran out and jumped into his arms. They kissed again and again. Both of them tried to speak at the same time. Her smile seemed to be sweeter and brighter than ever. Kurt brought his bag in and said hello to everyone.

Christmas Together

There were not a lot of plans for the rest of the week. If it had been up to Kurt and Mary, they would have found a private place and ignored everyone else. Kurt knew it would be rude, but it felt so good to have Mary in his arms again after nearly a month. She glowed, and he suspected that he did as well.

The family brought Kurt up to date on some of the proceedings. Bob had helped Sam find a job. Sam, Nancy, and Little Sammy were getting settled in. The same was true of Mrs. Johnson, Mary, and Joey. Mary and Kurt exchanged glances that told him she was not. She was making the best of a bad situation.

Bob asked, "I hear you got accepted at the University of Illinois. It's a great school. I loved it there. Do you know where your housing will be?"

"I requested Townsend Hall on Illinois Street. I don't know if that was a good choice or not. There were some things I liked about it."

"I lived in the Six Pack. It's handy to the stadium and the business classes, but it doesn't have air-conditioning like Townsend."

"Yes. I overheated during football practice two years ago, so air-conditioning is important. I hope I like it. I got two scholarships, which will help with the finances. Mom and Dad told me they can only help a little, so it's mainly up to me to pay."

"I got a tuition waiver scholarship for being the son of a World War II veteran. But of course, with Dad dying, I had to work and save my money to get through. Mom certainly didn't have the money to pay for me."

"I got the same scholarship. At least I know it can be done after talking to you. Thanks."

After a while, the conversation died down a little. Kurt found out he would be sleeping on the sofa. This was a considerable upgrade from a sleeping bag on the floor, and he was happy. Some of the family had errands to run. It was suggested that Kurt and Mary go for a drive, so she could show him around the city a bit.

They left, and Mary showed Kurt her high school. They also drove by Joey's school. Then they stopped at a mall. They could walk around together for a while, holding hands. Mary shared her fears and some of the good things that had happened since the move, but mainly how happy she was to see Kurt. He talked to her about how he missed her and how glad he was to be with her.

After a couple of hours, they went back home. When they got there, Kurt gave Mary her Christmas gift. She loved the necklace and gave him his gift. It was a cream-colored shirt with a blue sweater vest. They thanked one another and again fell into hugging and kissing. That night, they had leftovers for dinner. As usual, Mary had done a lot of the cooking for Christmas. The food was delicious. After dinner, Bob announced what he thought was a great find. It was a bottle of red wine named Johnson Vineyards. He wanted everyone to try it. He explained it was not a great wine but quite good for the price. Mainly, he liked the name.

Everyone came to get a glass except Kurt. Bob said, "Come on, Kurt. This is for the family. I'll only give you a swallow, and I promise you won't get drunk."

Kurt had never had a drink of alcohol before. A part of him didn't want to, but Bob was the one member of the family who seemed to like him. He came and got a glass with a small serving poured by Bob. After giving Kurt his glass, Bob made a toast to the Johnson family, and everyone drank the wine. Kurt drank it but did not like it.

After a little more visiting, Sam and his family went home. Everyone else got ready for bed. Kurt and Mary were left alone in the living room. They sat on the sofa and talked. As they did so, with Kurt's arm around Mary, her head leaning against his chest, they found themselves lying side by side, spooning. They made out for a while. They would talk for one moment, spend the next holding one another, and the next kissing. They lost all track of time.

Then they heard a noise. It was Mrs. Johnson. She'd walked in on them.

"Mary Elizabeth Johnson, come to my room!"

It was most definitely a command. Kurt sat up and tried to

hide his embarrassment. Mary went into her mother's room and he waited. Thirty minutes later, she came out and went to Kurt.

He started to apologize, but she held her fingers to his lips. "Mom said I am not to do that sort of thing. I told her we hadn't done anything inappropriate, but she didn't believe me. If she sees anything like that again, you are to leave and never return."

"So she isn't kicking me out tonight?"

Mary smiled. "No, you aren't out on the streets yet. But she was serious. We'll have to be better about controlling ourselves. We can do it, but I want you to be close to me."

Kurt turned red. "I feel like I'll die if I can't touch you. I want you in every way. But I've always been a good boy. I'm getting a little weary because of how I feel about you. But I would never want to do anything to bring shame to you. As frustrating as it is, I've got to be a little stronger."

They kissed good night, and Mary went to bed. Kurt prepared the sofa and lay down on it to go to sleep. He had a million thoughts running through his mind and had trouble falling asleep.

When morning came, Kurt was embarrassed around the rest of the Johnson family. Mary seemed tense. Her shoulders were hiked up. *I think Mary's as nervous as I am.* It seemed as though Mrs. Johnson had informed the entire family that there had been some "inappropriate" behavior the night before. She did it through hushed whispers and glances. As the day wore on, it began to get a little less uncomfortable. But the feeling was like a gray cloud hanging over their heads. At one point, Kurt and Mary heard Mrs. Johnson asking the other family members if they had any idea when "that boy" was leaving. Someone replied Kurt was leaving on Sunday, just like Lori and Terry.

After lunch, most of the family went to see where Sam and Nancy lived and ran a few errands. It was decided that Mary and Kurt would babysit Joey, Lisa, and Little Sammy. Mrs. Johnson said she would stay home "in case they needed help." Kurt and

Mary enjoyed this. Joey was busy playing with several of his Christmas presents. Lisa was intelligent and wanted them to take turns reading books to her. She was a fun, bright little treat.

Little Sammy was crawling around well at this stage. The hardest part of babysitting was keeping a close enough eye on him to prevent him from getting into danger. Kurt got on the floor with Little Sammy while Mary read to Lisa. As usual, Little Sammy wanted Kurt's glasses. They played and wrestled on the floor for quite a while. Finally, it was time for Little Sammy to take a nap. Mary took charge of this, and Kurt took over reading to Lisa. The only negative thing about the afternoon was that Mrs. Johnson was sitting in a recliner watching Kurt and Mary, like Madame Defarge, the entire time.

On Friday evening, Kurt and Mary decided to catch a movie. There wasn't anything playing they wanted to see. But they needed to get out of the house. They drove for about twenty minutes to the Circle Theater downtown. It was right on the Circle, across from the Veterans' Memorial. The theater itself was huge. In its day, it had been quite the place. It was decorated with large columns, arches, high vaulted ceilings, and stucco walls. However, by this time, it had seen better days and was not being kept up. They could almost feel the decay that had set in on a once beautiful facility.

The Man with the Golden Gun, the latest James Bond film with Roger Moore, was playing. The theater was so large you didn't need to sit within twenty seats of anyone else. Attendance was small. Kurt and Mary didn't care about any of that. The ability to have a degree of privacy was a huge plus. They were glad to sit without anyone staring. Kurt had his arm around Mary's shoulder; she placed her hand in his. They were able to enjoy being together.

On the way home from the movie, Kurt apologized for getting Mary in trouble with her mother. Mary's eyes flashed.

"She's never worried about anything like that. She's just trying to scare you away."

"So you don't want me to leave early? I was afraid you did."

"Not at all. I've looked forward to this for a month. I won't let her ruin it. Do you want to leave?"

"No. I want to be with you all the time. I just wanted to be sure I wasn't making things harder for you."

"My family is what is making life hard for me. You're my lifeline. The only thing I want is for us to be together. I do the cooking, the cleaning, the laundry, and the babysitting. I think she's afraid you'll take me away from her, and she'll have to find another way to get things done." There was a lot of anger and bitterness in Mary's voice.

"I would love to take you away from all that. I wish I could. We have to be patient. And you know I hate being patient."

Mary laughed. "Probably not as much as I do. But you're right. I'm glad you're here."

"I wish I could stay forever."

They pulled in front of the house and went inside. Things were a little less awkward that night. Sam and Nancy had gone home for the evening. Lori discussed her political ideas with Terry and Bob, but they weren't listening. Mrs. Johnson and the kids were all in bed. The five of them sat up talking for quite a while. It had turned into a lovely evening.

The conversation broke up, and everyone went to bed. Kurt and Mary were careful to say good night, kiss, and go their separate ways for the night. After a long while, Kurt dozed off. Worrying about Mrs. Johnson and what she thought of him was becoming a full-time job.

Saturday started well. Terry wanted to go to the annual Indianapolis Auto Show. Today was the grand opening of the event. After talking it over, it was decided that Terry, Lori, Bob, Sam, Mary, and Kurt would go. Nancy stayed with Mrs. Johnson and watched the children. They left to go to the show after lunch.

Once again, Kurt was overwhelmed by everything there. Mazda promoted its rotary engine, a new and unusual innovation in automobile engines. Mazda had introduced it a few years before and was pushing hard to build a market. They had an engine on display, which allowed Kurt to see its design theory and inner workings.

Another different vehicle was a full-sized conversion van. These had become very popular. This one had a beautiful exterior with a mural painted on the side panels. The interior contained all sorts of extras, and the rear seat converted into a bed, cupholders all over the place, shag carpet on the floor, and a quadraphonic sound system. It was interesting to look at. *That's so impractical.*

Two cars caught Kurt and Mary's attention. The first was a Fiat 124 convertible. It was bright red, with red-and-black-plaid seats and black trim. Sitting in the car, you felt like you were going fast while just sitting still.

The second was a Triumph TR 6. This was a royal blue convertible with a black interior. Kurt could picture Mary riding down the highway with him in this car, and it became a fantasy of his to someday own one.

There were hundreds of vehicles to see. Some were very ordinary, and others were beautiful works of art. The Jaguar E type was a pretty car, but the price was well over $10,000. Even in his dreams, this car wouldn't fit. Besides, he could buy two TR 6s for that money. For the rest of his life, he was fascinated by the TR 6.

Everyone had a good time at the auto show. When they got home, it was time for dinner. There was supposed to be a concert in a different part of Indianapolis that wasn't sold out that night. They could get tickets at the door. Bob gave Mary and Kurt directions on how to get there.

The two of them headed out, looking forward to a fun evening. About halfway there, the divided highway they were on was closed. After exiting, they tried to find a street that ran parallel. The one they chose came to a dead end. After backtracking, they tried two or three different ways and ended up lost.

They weren't sure where they were or how to get out. Mary didn't know the area of Indianapolis they were trying to go to. Neither did she know the area where they were lost. It looked like a rough neighborhood. There were bars, pool halls, and some exotic dancing venues. They decided to head in one direction and see if they could find a major thruway. When they did, they finally got their bearings, but having wasted nearly two hours driving around, they headed home.

When they got there, they watched an old movie on television. Lori walked in and asked why they were home so early. Mary explained about getting lost. Lori muttered something like, "Sure." She sat and kept casting dirty looks at Kurt.

After ten minutes of this, Lori left the room. Mrs. Johnson stayed up and viewed the movie with them. Kurt noticed she kept glancing at him. Finally, it was time for bed. Mrs. Johnson headed to her room. Kurt and Mary shared some warm embraces and kisses. Mrs. Johnson opened her door and came back down the hallway. Kurt and Mary had separated when she returned to the living room.

Everyone went to bed. Kurt fell asleep a little faster that night. It had been a nice day other than getting lost. Even that had been fun, especially after they found their way home. It had been a good day.

Sunday morning was gray and rainy. A gloom hung over Kurt and Mary. Kurt planned to leave after lunch. Every tick of the clock seemed a relentless weight piling on his shoulders. He played with Little Sammy for a while. He and Mary slipped off into the laundry room for a few minutes.

Mary gave Kurt a few eight tracks that belonged to him.

"Would you mind if I kept the Eagles and Guess Who tapes you have in the car?"

"You can have them; keep the ones you've got and anything else in the car. So far as I'm concerned, they're yours as much as mine." They shared that they had enjoyed the last few days. Each said they loved the other. Both were tearful. After a long embrace, they kissed and slipped back into the family room. Kurt went to the bathroom to wash his face. Mary returned to her room to regain her composure.

They found themselves in the living room a few minutes later and sat with one another on the sofa. As the time passed, they held hands without letting go. Each was holding the other's hand for dear life. Lunch came all too quickly. Kurt couldn't even remember whether he had eaten anything. After the meal, he said goodbye to everyone and took his bags to his car. Mary followed him. They had another lingering goodbye. It was reminiscent of the one on Thanksgiving Day. Kurt got in his car and drove off. Mary stood and watched until he turned the corner and was out of sight before returning to the house.

For the first few hours, Kurt could barely see as he drove along. The rain, the gray skies, and the tears that refused to stop made everything a blur. He pulled over a few times to try and regain his composure, but it only lasted a few minutes. Finally, about halfway home, he was all cried out.

Kurt had to stop and buy some gasoline about an hour from home. When he got ready to leave the service station, his car wouldn't start. The battery had died. He was able to jump-start it with some cables the station had available. When he got home, he shut off the engine and tried to restart the car. The battery was dead. It was a lousy end to a bad day.

When he came into the house, his parents were waiting for him. They were glad he'd made it home. They ordered a pizza for dinner. After showering, Kurt had pizza. They asked him about the trip. He told them most of what happened. He didn't mention the incident with Mrs. Johnson on the first night or getting lost in the wrong part of town. He did talk with his father about his car. The alternator was going bad. With Tuesday being New Year's Eve, it would probably be at least Thursday or Friday of the following week before the alternator could be replaced. So Kurt was without wheels for the next week. He was exhausted from the drive and the emotional strain of the day.

Kurt went to bed early but couldn't sleep. He wished he was still in Indianapolis and that Mary had not moved away. Mary's birthday was in the second to last week of January. Kurt decided to ask his parents if he could visit Mary the weekend before or the weekend after her birthday. He would wait a few days to ask. He turned on the radio and listened to music until he fell asleep.

The next day, Kurt slept until ten. When he came downstairs, he skipped breakfast. Kurt volunteered to do a few chores around the house for his mother. He swept the carpets and did the laundry from his trip. Later in the day, Racket dropped by when he saw Kurt's car was back home. He agreed to pick him up and hang out that night. Tuesday was New Year's Eve. Kurt didn't feel like celebrating anything. He cruised with Roger Sloan, but they both went home early.

Chapter 8
1975 Begins

Trying Hard

Wednesday morning, school started. The schedule he enjoyed so much when he spent three periods with Mary no longer interested him. Homeroom began at 8:20 a.m. At the beginning of the school year, Kurt was at school by 8:00 a.m. That gave him fifteen or more minutes to spend with Mary, walk her to her homeroom, and get to his. Now, he set his alarm for 7:55 a.m. He dressed, ran downstairs, grabbed breakfast, brushed his teeth, combed his hair, and hurried to school. He ran into homeroom just at the bell.

When Kurt got home from school on Wednesday, he had two pieces of good news: his car was fixed, and he had a letter from Mary. He paid his dad for the cost of the alternator and labor. Then he went up to his room with Mary's letter. He opened it. The words he read were not what he expected.

Dear Kurt,

The last few days have been hard for me. After you drove away on Sunday, I went to my room. I needed some time to finish crying. Now I know how you felt when I drove off on Thanksgiving Day. Then I washed my face and went to the family room. Mom and Lor were the only ones there.

Mom complained that you were here four days and only took me out one night. I said you were only here three nights and took me out twice. We couldn't help it that we got lost.

Then Lori started complaining about the auto show. When we got there, Terry paid for six tickets. Later, Bob paid Terry back for his and Sam's tickets. She said you never even offered to pay. Lori called you a cheapskate. I asked Lori why Terry bought the tickets if he didn't want to pay. Most people would have bought their tickets and let everyone else buy their own. Terry didn't even care about the money. Lori was trying to find things to tear you down. Mom joined in and said you never spent much money on me. They both claimed that if you liked me, you would be willing to do more things for me and spend more on me.

I told them you didn't make a big show of the things you do for me. There was the time when you surprised me with those earrings. You bought an album for me. For homecoming, you gave me rosebuds instead of a cheap carnation. I mentioned how you were always buying treats for Joey. The week we moved, you took me to the nicest restaurant in the area. You always did special things for me and spent as much money on me as I ever cared about. But they wouldn't listen.

Then Mom brought up Thursday night. She said she was shocked when she walked in and found us having sex on the sofa. I told her we weren't having sex. We were hugging and kissing. Mom yelled, "I know what I saw!"

She said that if that was all you were after, I was better off without
you. Mom told me that if I couldn't control myself any better than that, I
didn't need to be seeing any boys. Lori butted in and said if that's all there
was to our relationship, I needed to stop dating you before I got pregnant.
That launched Mom into orbit. She said she raised me to know better
than that, and I ought to be ashamed.

It just went on and on. I was crying. They were yelling the most
hateful things. At first, I tried to argue with them. You're the nicest
boy I've ever dated. You cared about me and tried to take care of me. I
said you were the only boy who ever asked me about Dad, Joey, and all
the rest. They wouldn't listen. I decided to be quiet and think about
how much I love you. After a little more than an hour, they were
through.

When they finished, I returned to my bedroom for the rest of the day.
At least until Mom yelled at me to prepare dinner; I cooked it but didn't
eat it. I just sat at the table until they were done to wash everything up.
Then I went to my room. Now I'm writing to tell you about it. I miss you
so much. I don't know how I'm going to get through this. Please call as
soon as you can. I need you.

I love you with all my heart,
Mary

Kurt was angry when he read the letter. His hands trembled, and
he bounced both legs so much that it shook the room. *How dare*
they do that to Mary. They bully her and try to rob her of any happiness.
It hadn't occurred to him to offer to repay Terry for the tickets. If
Terry didn't want to pay, Kurt thought he would have only paid
for two tickets and let the other men pay for theirs. Kurt had
apologized to Mary about getting lost and the fiasco with her
mother the first night.

Then he began to wonder if he had done anything wrong.
Maybe this was his fault. He knew he was lucky that Mary even
considered dating him. *I must beg Mary's forgiveness if I haven't*

treated her well. If this is my fault, I've got to make it up to her. He wrote all this in a letter and sent it the following day.

Dear Mary,

I'm so sorry you had to go through that. When I read your last letter, I got so angry I couldn't stand it. I was mad at them for ambushing you and attacking you. I was upset about the things they said about me. After rereading your letter, I want to tell you that if I did anything wrong, I apologize from the bottom of my heart. Please forgive me. If I need to do something to make things right with your mother or Lori, please tell me what I should do. I'd be lost without you. I should never have done anything that would put you in that position.

I'm not trying to justify myself, but it never occurred to me to pay Terry. I was surprised when he paid for everyone, but I assumed he did that because he wanted to. I had my wallet out to buy our tickets, and he waved us all in and said he'd bought them. I can send him a check if you think I should. I've already apologized for Thursday night. It had been so long since we'd been together; it was wonderful to hold you. I probably am too tight with money. I try not to be. I know that you deserve the best. Please be honest with me and tell me if I've failed you.

Regarding the night we got lost, do they believe I got lost on purpose and drove around in the wrong part of town for an hour to keep from going somewhere with you and having fun? You were disappointed that night. I don't blame you. I was disappointed too.

Please tell me what I can do to help you. I'm so sorry if I've brought this on you. I love you more than I believed I could ever love anyone— more than I know how to say.

With all my love,
Kurt

He couldn't wait for a reply, so he called Mary on Saturday evening to talk with her. He was nervous as he dialed. Would

Mary answer? Her mother? What would he say to Mrs. John-son? Someone answered the phone.

Mary said, "Hello."

"It's so good to hear your voice. I'm sorry you've had such a bad week. Are you all right?"

"I got your letter. It helped. I read some of it to Mom. I reminded her that Lori hadn't liked you since I told her friend from Paducah that I was dating you. I don't know if it helped, but Mom hasn't said anything since I did that."

"If any of this was my fault, please tell me. I would never want to hurt you."

"I talked to Bob. He helped me a lot. He asked me when the last time that Mom liked anyone I'd dated was. Bob even told Mom that he liked you and that you're the nicest boy I'd ever gone out with."

"I'm glad you have Bob with you. I like him too. Do you think your mother would let me come and visit you close to your birthday? I would probably stay on Friday and Saturday nights. I have to talk to my parents about it though."

"I don't know, but I'll ask. I hope you can come."

"I don't know if it will be the weekend before or after your birthday. Wait until I've got it cleared with my folks. There's no use in pushing your mom about something until we know I can do it."

"That sounds like an excellent plan to me. I'm feeling better about everything now. I miss you."

They continued to talk for about thirty minutes. The longer they talked, the more they relaxed. Both felt better when they hung up.

At dinner on Sunday, Kurt asked his father, "Could I go and visit Mary toward the end of the month? It's her birthday."

"I'm not sure your car is up to it, son. You had trouble on the way home at Christmas."

"Yes, but we got that fixed. I haven't had any problems since.

The weather has been worse for the last week than for that trip. I think my car will be fine."

Mrs. Kellerman said, "We have special church events on both Sundays. You can't skip those."

"Mom, neither of those special events involves me. One is for the women's group for missions, and the other is a special day for teenage girls. Nobody will care if I'm there or not. I hardly ever miss church."

"I don't know about that, but I agree with your mother. You can't be driving up to Indianapolis every three weeks. That's just out of the question."

"I'm not asking to drive there every three weeks. I asked to do it for Christmas and Mary's birthday. I can't help that they're only a month apart. You've often seen Judy on Christmas and turned around to see her on her birthday in the first week of January. She lives all the way up in Chicago. I don't mean to argue with you about this, but you're wrong."

"Son, we've made our decision. No, you will not be going to Indianapolis. That's settled. Don't ask about it again."

Kurt never argued with his parents. But he felt they were wrong and said so.

Kurt thought he would wait and try again. He didn't think they would change their minds, but he had to try. He struggled to figure out what was happening. His parents had liked Mary, but now it seemed they weren't supportive.

They corresponded with one another, writing twice a week. Some letters were in reply to one another. Others passed each other in the mail. Kurt knew that whenever he saw a yellow envelope on the kitchen table when he got home, his heart beat faster and he dropped everything to read the letter as soon as possible.

His parents were firm when he brought up the idea of seeing Mary for her birthday again. The issue was decided. This was final. Kurt was not happy. He couldn't accept his parents' reasoning on this. But he'd always been taught to obey. The Bible was very clear on this. So how did a Christian handle the obligation to obey his parents when they were wrong? Kurt felt he couldn't disobey them on this.

The next day, his father wanted to talk to him. "Son, the phone bill came today. There is one call to Indianapolis that cost nearly forty dollars. That's not acceptable. If you make one call every month, along with taxes and fees, it will cost us over five hundred dollars for the year. I work hard to provide for our family. But that means half of one month's pay each year is for nothing but you to talk to some girl."

"Dad, I understand that. It isn't fair to you. But I work hard and save my money. I'll pay you for the phone call, the taxes, and the fees. Just tell me what I owe you. That's only fair."

"No. I don't want your money. I'm telling you not to make expensive phone calls like that anymore."

On Thursday night, Kurt went to visit Racket. Racket worked at a filling station on the edge of town most weeknights. There was a phone booth at the station. Kurt brought a roll of quarters and called Mary. He told her the bad news about coming for her birthday.

Mary took it better than he expected. She'd brought it up with her mother, and Mrs. Johnson said it was too soon for another visit. Nothing was going their way, but hearing one another's voices was fantastic. Mary talked about school. She was getting used to it, although she wished she was back home. Kurt spoke about being closer to her in August when he started college, and somehow, they would be able to see one another. He shared gossip about some of their friends to bring Mary up to date. They were very happy, and time seemed to fly. They finally said goodbye and hung up.

Kurt paid nine dollars for the first three minutes when he placed the call. After three minutes, the operator came on and asked for $4.50 for another three. She didn't come on anymore.

A few seconds after he hung up, the pay phone began to ring. Racket told him not to answer it. Kurt felt like it would be better if he did. He picked up the receiver. It was the operator.

"Please insert $48.00 for the remainder of your call."

"Wow! Um, I need a minute to get the coins. Don't hang up. I'll be right back."

He got change from Racket (including a twenty-dollar loan).

"Hello. I have the coins now."

"Please insert $48.00."

It took a few minutes to feed $48.00 in quarters into the slot. "Ma'am? What would have happened if I hadn't answered the phone after the call was over?"

"The charges would be reversed to the other party, along with a 10 percent penalty and fees."

"Thank you for the information. Goodbye."

Kurt was relieved he'd taken care of it. He could imagine Mrs. Johnson's reaction if she'd received a sixty-dollar bill for Kurt's call. Besides, it was the right thing to do. The problem was that Kurt couldn't afford to make a call like that often.

Kurt and Mary kept on writing letters. Occasionally, Kurt would call Mary, and once in a while, Mary would call Kurt. Their love for one another was as strong as ever. They would not allow difficulties to stop them.

On her birthday, Mary called Kurt on her way home from school. She knew he couldn't pay for another call, and she could only afford three minutes. He wished her a happy birthday, and they pledged their love to one another. It was just important for her to hear his voice on her birthday. After they hung up, Kurt was heartbroken about how alone Mary must be. *If only there were something I could do to help her.* He did his best to show his love and help her through a difficult time.

In February Kurt received a surprise phone call from Mary. She was going to be able to come visit her grandmother, who still lived back home. She would arrive late on Friday night and be in town on Valentine's Day. Kurt nearly exploded with joy. He spent the day with her on Saturday and took her out Saturday evening. They were so happy to be together; saying goodbye was not nearly as painful this time. It would not be easy, but they could get through this.

They continued in this fashion for months. Mary made it down again in March and once more in April. Kurt could call for five or ten minutes monthly from home and once every six weeks from a pay phone. His savings dwindled, but if that was the only way he could talk to Mary, what choice did he have? The letters flowed. Some were sweet and profound; some expressed the frustrations that happen in daily life. But they both knew that one day, things would be better.

Kurt Fails a Test

As the end of the school year grew near, Kurt called Mary in late April. After some general conversation, Kurt brought up the main point of the call.

"Is there any way that you can go to prom with me? It's the first Saturday night in May."

"Of course. I'll talk to Mom and Bob and get it all arranged. I'm looking forward to it. The prom up here is the second Saturday in May. Would you come to it? I want my friends at school to meet you."

"I'll talk to my parents and get it squared away. I can't wait to see you."

The next day, Kurt made a reservation for two with the prom committee. It was a fee that was refunded if you stayed at prom until it was over. Things were getting better. That evening, Kurt asked his father. "Dad, Mary is coming down here to go to prom with me in a few weeks. She's traveled down here three times since Christmas; this will be the fourth. Her prom at her new school is one week after the prom here. May I please go to her prom? I haven't asked to go there since her birthday, and I wasn't allowed to go then. I would appreciate it. It's important to me."

"Well, son, I'll think about it. Let me talk about it with your mother. You're right; you haven't asked since January. I'll get back to you in a few days."

He didn't say no. He's going to let me go. I'm going to see Mary two weekends in a row. I knew if I did the right thing and showed respect for them, Mom and Dad would finally come around.

On the Tuesday before prom, the phone rang, and Kurt answered. It was Mary. She was in tears.

"What's wrong, Mary?"

"I'm sorry, but I won't be able to go to the prom with you this weekend. Bob has an important client that needs something right away. He can't bring me down."

"I'm sorry too. But don't worry about it. Everything will be fine."

"Are you coming up here next week?"

"I think so. I asked Dad, and he said he'd get back to me. If he was going to say no, he would've come right out with it. He's not home right now. I'll find out and call you in the next couple of days. I'm sure it's okay."

Shortly after the call ended, Kurt's parents got home. They expressed sympathy when he told them that Mary couldn't make it. His mother carried on that it wasn't right for someone to miss his senior prom. "Kurt, you should take a friend and go to the prom anyway."

"No, Mom. If I can't take Mary, I don't care about going."

"Your senior prom is special. It's the last time you'll be together with a lot of your classmates. You shouldn't miss that. It doesn't have to be a girlfriend. It can just be a friend. You'll regret it the rest of your life if you don't go."

"It might be special to a lot of people, Mom. Not to me though. The only reason I was going was because I figured

Mary's family would bring her down for something like prom. Her brother can't bring her because of work, so there's no point."

"But you paid a twenty-dollar deposit. You'll lose that money. It's silly not to go. You'll have a nice meal and spend the evening with your friends. I know Jacquie from church would go with you. She's two or three years older than you. No one would think of her as a date for you. It would just be two friends. She's a nice girl. She knows Mary. That would be good for you."

He didn't care about prom though. For him, it meant nothing without Mary. On Thursday, he came home from school, and his mother smiled. She'd called Jacquie, who had agreed to go to prom with Kurt as a friend. His mother kept pushing him until he agreed.

The moment he said this, Kurt knew he had messed up. He tried to think of a way out of it. He asked his mother to call and cancel since she had given the invitation. She refused and told him he was not to call and cancel either. Kurt felt sick to his stomach. This had to be wrong.

That night, Mary called again. Bob had altered his schedule to bring Mary down for the prom. Kurt told his parents. They both insisted he honor the commitment he'd agreed to with Jacquie. Struggling, Kurt told Mary he was committed to taking someone else as a friend. He could hear the pain in Mary's voice.

She said, "Can you come to my prom next weekend?"

Kurt realized his father had never given him an answer. He asked his parents. They said, "No! It's Mother's Day. You're going with us to visit your brother in Jefferson City and make it a nice day for your mother!"

Kurt yelled, "You haven't let me see Mary in over four months! I told her I couldn't take her to my prom! You've got to let me go to her!"

Kurt saw his father get angry with him for the first time in his life. Mr. Kellerman said, "You've heard our decision. You are not going to Indianapolis! You will go with us and celebrate Mother's Day with your own family. That's the end of it!"

Kurt went back to the phone. Mary said, "I heard some shouting. What's going on?"

"I can't come. I don't know what to do. They won't let me go to your prom."

Mary tearfully said goodbye. Then she hung up.

Kurt ran out of the house and walked down the railroad tracks for several miles. He didn't know what to do. His only choices were to obey his parents and hurt Mary or to disobey them and head out for Indianapolis in a week. If he did that, he was leaving home for good. This meant he could forget about the University of Illinois. As a high school graduate, he could make at most $70–75 per week if he went to work. That was less than $4,000 per year. He couldn't support Mary on that. He thought November 28 was the worst day of his life. He was wrong. It was May 1.

He turned around and walked back toward home. When he got there, he took off in his car. He was driving ninety miles an hour down the highway. His car wouldn't go any faster than that. The engine whined. As Kurt steered around a sharp curve, he lost control and slid off the pavement at the end of the curve. The car spun in circles in the grass on the side of the road. He'd taken his foot off the accelerator after he left the highway. He came to a stop.

He looked around. Somehow the car had missed a couple of signposts and a tree. The car was undamaged. His heart raced, and he felt as though he would throw up. He pushed on the accelerator, and the car moved. He wasn't stuck. Kurt pulled back onto the highway and drove home. His life was over. He couldn't defy his parents and run away from home. But that was the only way to keep Mary. But how long could he keep Mary if he was a homeless pauper? *I wish I'd hit the tree when the car left the road. Then it wouldn't matter.*

Kurt took Jacquie to the prom. He barely spoke to her all night. They didn't dance a single time. He left early and forfeited his deposit. He dropped her off at her house, thanked her, and went home. She had been kind and polite but left him alone.

When Kurt got home, he went to bed but didn't sleep. When the time came, he got up, got ready, and went to church. He didn't talk to anyone and spent the morning staring off into nowhere. After church, he had a few bites of food and left the table. Still unable to sleep, he went for a drive. His mind worked feverishly the entire time, trying to figure out what to do.

One week ago, Kurt's life was well planned. He would graduate from high school, see Mary a few times over the summer, and go to university in the fall, and from there, he had a few options. He could buy Mary an engagement ring for her eighteenth birthday or high school graduation. If she wanted him to finish school before getting married, he would. If she wanted to marry while he was still attending school, he would. They would have children, raise a family of several, and be happy.

Every single part of the plan was in jeopardy now. He ran one scenario after another. Should he rebel against his parents, buy a ring, and go propose to Mary now? Should he obey his parents and see how things worked out? Should he wait and react to whatever happened next? There were dozens of possibilities.

After more than thirty hours without sleep, Kurt made a decision. He needed to send a letter to Mary. He needed to play by the rules and do the right thing. He'd always been taught and believed that if you do the right thing, somehow things would work out.

The Fatal Letter

Kurt sat and wrote a letter to Mary.

Dear Mary,

I am ever so sorry for everything that happened. I'm sorry I hurt you. That's the one thing I never meant to do. It was entirely my fault. I want you to know the girl I took to prom is just a friend and nothing more. I promise.

But since I took someone out, it is only right and fair that you feel free to go out with someone if you choose to. It's not fair for you to be trapped and alone in Indianapolis.

I will call you soon. Please write. I love you more than life itself. Please come down here as quickly as possible. I miss you so badly I feel like I could die. I'll call you very soon. Again, I apologize and ask you to forgive me.

With all my love,
Kurt

There were some things about his reasoning that Kurt did not explain in the letter. Kurt realized his parents would never permit him to go to Indianapolis. He felt foolish that he hadn't realized it earlier. Every time he asked after the Christmas visit, the answer was no. It wasn't right or fair that the only way he and Mary could see one another was for her to make the five-hour trip.

He mailed the letter the following day. Kurt pinned all of his hopes on Mary forgiving him. He knew that whatever happened over the summer, once he was away at school, he could call her. He could also catch a bus from Champaign to Indianapolis at a reasonable price and visit her. He wouldn't need his parents' permission to do that. If he could keep their relationship alive until August 15, he knew somehow things would work out.

Kurt fell asleep around nine on Sunday night and slept until eight the following day. He went to school, but nothing was the same. He didn't want to see or talk to anyone. He hoped for a yellow envelope in the mail daily, but there wasn't one. He skipped the end-of-the-year sports banquet. Later he discovered he'd been awarded trophies for Most Valuable Player and Most Tackles in football. He didn't care.

His parents dragged him to his brother's house for Mother's Day weekend. No one talked to Kurt, and he just moped around. Kurt was thinking of home. He wondered if Mary had gone to her prom with someone. If she would ever speak to him again. It all seemed so bleak.

Kurt went to the service station where Tracker worked one night to place a phone call. After paying nine dollars for the first three minutes, he heard Mrs. Johnson's voice. "What do you want?"

"I would like to speak to Mary, please."

"She doesn't want to speak to you. Don't you bother her anymore!"

Kurt felt the wind knocked out of him. He couldn't breathe. He was sure Mary would at least speak to him. "Please let me speak to her. I want to apologize to her, to you, and Bob. Please give me another chance."

"No! She isn't here and wouldn't want to talk to you if she was! Goodbye! Don't ever bother us again!"

She hung up. Kurt had expected trouble but didn't think it would be this bad. He thought it over and was sure Mary had been home. She probably didn't want to speak to him, but he would try again in a week. It was only nine dollars, so he would have plenty left to try again.

Graduation was coming in a few days, but that was the least of Kurt's concerns. He continued to write letters to Mary, telling her of his plans. He wanted her to be sure of his intentions. He tried to explain the reason for the letter after the prom. Since Indianapolis was on eastern standard time all year long, he could call later in the evening than in the winter. Then Mrs. Johnson would be in bed, and Mary would answer the phone.

Kurt decided to give it another try. He returned to the same old phone booth, dialed, and paid. With all his heart, Kurt prayed that Mary would answer the phone. It started ringing, and every muscle in his body tensed. Someone lifted the receiver.

"Hello." Kurt heard Mrs. Johnson's voice.

"Hello. This is Kurt Kellerman, Mrs. Johnson. May I please speak to Mary?"

"Why?"

"Because I want to tell her how sorry I am for everything that's happened. I want her to know how much I care about her. I want to beg her forgiveness."

"Well, she doesn't want to hear any of your lies! You've caused her enough trouble already. I'm glad she's rid of you. Now don't you call back anymore. Goodbye!" She hung up.

Kurt was at a total loss. He continued to write to her, but his begging and pleading on the telephone were going nowhere. It seemed his plans were not working, as there were no replies to his letters. *Is there anything else I can do? What could it be?*

Kurt went through graduation, but it was just a blur. His family was there to see him. He didn't care. There were several graduation parties that night, but none interested Kurt. When his sister asked him if he was getting together with any friends, he said that he was and left the house. He took off in his car and drove out into the country. He stopped at a cemetery and parked. Then he got out and walked around. All he wanted was to be with Mary. He just wanted to be alone if he couldn't be with her.

He walked around until nearly midnight. It was the only

place he could be sure no one would bother him. Kurt hoped everyone would be in bed before he got home. When he got back to the house, the only lights on were in the family room. He slipped in and saw that everyone was in bed except his father.

Kurt sneaked into the bathroom and then padded into the family room. His father was asleep on his favorite recliner with the television turned on. Kurt turned the television off, which caused his father to jerk his head up.

"What's going on? Why'd you turn off the TV?"

"Dad, I got home, and you were asleep. I was just turning the TV off and going to bed. Good night." He hoped that his father wouldn't want to talk. Kurt just wanted to go to bed and end a horrible day. Fortunately, his father didn't feel like chatting and let him go upstairs to bed.

Kurt fell on his bed and looked out the window at the stars in the sky. He turned on the radio and hoped it would help him fall asleep like the television did his father. It seemed that the events of the last month just played over and over in his mind. He fell into a restless slumber, filled with dreams of phone calls where Mrs. Johnson yelled at him. There were other dreams where Mary told him how much she hated him. When he woke up, he felt more tired than before he'd gone to bed. Hopefully, things would get better. Kurt didn't see how they could get worse.

Chapter 9
The Long Summer

Disappointment after Disappointment

K urt worked at the hardware store over the summer. He also umpired baseball games for the various leagues at the local sports complex during the evenings. When he wasn't working, he hung out with his friends. He worked most of the time that summer, trying to earn and save as much money as possible before heading to college.

As per his plan, he continued writing letters to Mary. Each day, with less hope, he looked for a yellow envelope with Mary's fluid writing. After two more phone calls, both answered by Mrs. Johnson and going just as badly as the earlier ones, he didn't call as often.

Kurt drove by Mary's house daily to see if anyone was there, but it was always empty. He also cruised by Mary's grandmother's house. The last time he kissed Mary and held her in his arms was on the front porch of that house in April. The possibility that Mary might come to see her grandmother never left his thoughts. He would go by the house at all hours of the day and night. But it never yielded any results.

On his birthday in late June, Kurt turned eighteen. But there was no celebration, no gifts, no cake. He didn't want anything. His relationship with his parents had deteriorated over the last two months. He still loved them but could not understand why they had treated Mary as they had.

On Independence Day, he and Racket went to see the fireworks together. Just as they were starting, a thunderstorm blew up. The fireworks were canceled, and everyone hurried to get out of the rain. He and Racket were both soaked. That was the extent of his social life for the summer.

Kurt did prepare to move to Urbana. He had his dorm assignment and his class schedule. One day he received a letter that he had proficiency tested out of some classes. That was the best news he received that summer.

As the summer wore on, Kurt became more and more surly. His temper was on edge. It was evident to his friends that he wasn't happy. His parents didn't see this at all.

One day, his mother asked why he wasn't going out with anyone. Kurt responded, "I'm not going out with anyone other than Mary. You won't let me go to Indianapolis, and she hasn't come down, so I guess I'll have to wait."

"If she got that angry over one date with a friend, she didn't care for you that much anyway."

Kurt flared up. His face was red. His hands shook.

"Don't ever say anything like that again! You set it up! You wouldn't let me go to her prom! You made me go to Jefferson City, where I didn't do anything. It was as if I wasn't even there the entire weekend. You didn't care if I went to Jefferson City over Mother's Day. You only cared that I did NOT go to Indianapolis to be with Mary! This isn't about one date. This is about never traveling to see her. It's about never doing something nice for her. This is about betraying her. Don't you ever say anything bad about her again! If you want to say something bad about me, I don't care. My life is ruined. And you did it!"

Kurt had never spoken to her like this in his life. A shocked silence fell over the house. He walked out of the house and went for a drive. He averaged more than eighty which put a strain on his car's engine. This time he didn't have any near misses.

July was approaching its end. Kurt's duties as an umpire would be over at the end of July. He would have more free time after that. Kurt dreaded it. Being busy helped him stay numb. In two weeks and a few days, he would be gone. He had mailed Mary his address and phone number for when he left for school and the date he was moving in. He kept crossing his fingers that things would change for the better.

The Futile Phone Call

On August 12, Kurt received a package from Indianapolis. He was excited and nervous. He recognized the handwriting. It was impossible to know the contents, but it was the first thing he'd received or heard from Mary since the first of May. It had been fourteen weeks since he'd heard anything from Mary. Kurt's hands shook so badly that he could barely open the package.

Inside were several things that either belonged to Kurt or that Kurt had given to Mary. There was also a letter. He opened the letter with a mixture of fear and hope.

Kurt,

I want to return these things. This should be everything that belonged to you. When you took another girl to prom, it ended our relationship. The prom was more important to you than I was.

Since then, I've moved on. I'm dating someone else now. He's good to me and spends a lot on me. He took me to an Eagles concert last week. Now that I'm dating him, I felt I should get these back to you.

Sincerely,

Mary

Tears blinded Kurt. His entire world had come undone. He went for a walk down the train tracks. Kurt needed to regain his composure. He needed to think. Even though the letter devastated him, there was hope. She mentioned the Eagles. His Eagles tape was one of the things she returned. She also mentioned spending *and being good to her. It was to wound me.* Kurt turned around and walked back home.

Kurt picked up the telephone. He dialed the number that he would still remember fifty years later. The phone rang. Mrs. Johnson answered. "Hello."

"Hello, Mrs. Johnson. This is Kurt again. I know you don't want to talk to me, but I am begging you to please allow me to speak to Mary."

"Mary doesn't want to talk to you. Why don't you give up and quit bothering us?"

"What you say might be true, but I must hear it from Mary. Please let me talk to Mary, even if she tells me she doesn't want to talk to me."

A moment later, Mary was on the phone. Hearing her voice made Kurt's heart pound. He struggled to maintain control of himself. Mary said, "What do you want?"

"I want to apologize. You can't imagine how sorry I am. Please forgive me."

"Have you enjoyed dating other people this summer?"

"I haven't been on any dates. The only time I went out with anyone was to the stupid prom dance, and we were only friends. We didn't dance, we didn't kiss, we didn't hold hands. She sat and watched me be miserable all night because she wasn't you. You are the only person I love, and I don't know how I can live without you. Please give me another chance. I'm begging you to forgive me."

"I don't think I can trust you anymore. You're going to be

busy with college. You need to save your money for that and not on phone calls to me. I've found someone else. He has plenty of money. He took me to see the Eagles last week. He's not worried about things like that. You're the one who wanted us to both date other people, so quit calling."

"I don't want us to date other people. You are the only person in the world for me. Please, please forgive me. Come back to me. I can't live without you."

"I'm sorry. Goodbye." There was a click, and the phone was dead.

Kurt left the house again and ran down the railroad tracks. He went to a quiet little place where a creek went under the tracks and sat to think. It was about two miles from town. He kept going over and over the conversation. Mary had been angry and hurt. She did not want to allow Kurt to hurt her again.

No. There was nothing to hope for in her words today. There was nothing to hope for in the letter he'd received. She clearly mentioned the guy, the Eagles concert, and the money to injure Kurt. Was there a possibility that given time, she might be able to vent her anger, and if Kurt showed himself to be trustworthy, she could forgive him and restore their relationship? Maybe. It was a long shot. He could only hope. He would call again after he was at school.

Kurt walked back home. He came in the door. "Mom! Dad! You know I got mail from Mary. You know I called Mary. That's all you need to know. I don't want to talk about it. Don't mention it. Bye." After that, he got in his car and came home late that night.

He moped around for the next few days, hoping he could find some way to make things right with Mary. He avoided most of his friends. He wanted to get out of town and start fresh. That meant getting back together with Mary. On Saturday, his parents drove him to Urbana, and he moved into his dorm room.

Chapter 10
The Plan

Hope for the Future

E ven though Kurt was all alone at a major university, he felt less lonely than he had over the summer. At least he could now make another effort regarding Mary. He continued to write her and expected no replies. But still, one could never be sure. The more he thought about the phone call of the previous week, the more he convinced himself that he had injured Mary in May. Despite all the letters he had sent since then, last week was the first time they had spoken to one another since Kurt had failed her.

Kurt knew he'd hurt Mary. She'd said a lot of things she didn't mean. He'd have to win her back. He'd begin by writing letters. He just needed to prove he was not going away. Kurt needed to let her know he would always be there.

So the first step would be to continue writing. He could now call less expensively. The money Kurt had saved over the summer would allow him to call Mary on the landline phone in his dorm room rather than from a pay phone. He could now phone at any hour of the day or night. So the second step was to plan and carry out a telephone offensive. Third, he needed to woo her. Kurt had to find ways to express his love that would be more effective than just words. Fourth, when the time was right, he would catch a bus to Indianapolis and show up at her front door, face-to-face.

Kurt gave little thought to the classes he took that first semester. This was just a better location to try and work things out with Mary. It had become clear to him since May that, for whatever reason, his parents opposed his relationship with Mary. They probably thought the young lovers were too serious at too young an age. Possibly they thought Kurt would get married and drop out of school, hurting his future career prospects. Perhaps they feared Mary would get pregnant and embarrass the family with a shotgun wedding. He didn't know. He just knew it was a problem for whatever reason. There was much greater freedom of action away from home.

Kurt was attentive to his finances. He had saved money to last through the school year, but he wanted to be able to finance his campaign to win Mary back. He didn't have a job at school. But around the second or third week in the dorm, he found a steady income source. Card playing was popular in the dorms. Kurt discovered he was terrible at poker and tended to lose. So he quit playing. On the other hand, the most popular game on his floor was playing Spades for a penny per point.

The rules were simple. He watched a few games. Then a sophomore who everyone called Spudich explained the rules while he watched a game between Wert, Crazy Rich, Ray, and Paul. "There are four players and no teams. Each player bids how many tricks he can take, with the dealer going last. You earn ten points for every trick you take if you get enough to cover your bid. Any additional tricks you take after you cover your bid are worth one point. There are no penalties for over-tricks; if you fail to make your bid, you earn negative ten points times your bid. A nil bid is worth fifty points if you don't take a single trick. It's minus fifty if you take any. You could lead spades any time, even on the first trick. Reaching 300 points ends the game. Each player pays or receives one penny per point from the others, rounded to the nearest nickel." Wert won the game they were watching. He and Paul made money. Crazy Rich broke even. Ray lost around four dollars.

The rules differed from those Kurt played at home, but he liked them. He played some games well, and he got thumped in a few. He watched others play and soon discovered the formula for success. By the end of the year, Kurt had the third-highest winnings out of seventy-plus Spades players.

With cash to finance his campaign, Kurt began to call Mary at least every two weeks. She now answered the phone and talked to him. By the end of September, he called once per week. She still told him to quit calling and save his money and that she was dating someone else, but she also kept answering the phone and talking for thirty minutes to an hour.

Kurt called on a Wednesday night in late September. Mary answered. "Hello."

"Hi, this is Kurt. Do you have time to talk to me?"

"Okay. These calls must cost a lot of money. You need to save it for school."

"I saved almost everything I earned over the summer and have a well-paying job here. There's nothing I'd rather spend my money on than you. How are you doing?"

"You know I'm still dating someone. School is okay. How are your classes?"

"They're all right. My main concern is you. Thank you for letting me talk to you. How is Joey? I miss him too. But not as much as you."

"He's fine. He's been really happy since we moved. It's funny sometimes when Lisa bosses him around. He tells her, 'You're not the boss of me,' just like he did with you." She laughed at this.

"We had a lot of fun babysitting him."

"Yes. You were a big help. No one else ever helped me babysit him. Thank you."

"I did it for you."

The conversation rambled on for thirty minutes. There was a definite softening. She laughed a few more times. Kurt's hope soared. They said goodbye. There was no "I love you." But she talked to him.

She never mentioned his letters, but he kept writing. He considered asking her why but didn't want to push his luck. If he was patient, things seemed to be going in the right direction.

Kurt decided to send her a gift. After much thought, he ordered a dozen long-stemmed red roses. He called that night.

"Thank you for the roses. They were beautiful."

"I'm glad you liked them. I remember the rosebud corsage I got you last October. You looked so beautiful. I always talk about the past. How was your day? What are you doing? Have you thought about what you're going to do after you graduate?"

"I think I might want to study nursing. What do you think about that?"

"You'd be a great nurse. You've been the primary caregiver for your mom for years. Then there's Joey, Lisa, and Little Sammy; you care for all ages. Mary, you're a very kind and compassionate person. It's one of the things I love about you."

They talked like this for three hours that night. When she said goodbye, she thanked him for calling. Kurt was excited. *She's finally coming around. I knew if I could talk to her, things would work out.* He started checking into bus fare to Indianapolis. It was reasonably cheap. He would also need cab fare and a place to stay, but he could do that with his winnings from playing cards.

Kurt talked to her two or three more times. She was less

hostile. Their conversations always lasted at least two to three hours. His roommate worked in one of the many libraries on campus during the evenings, so he had plenty of privacy. He kept emphasizing how much he loved Mary. He tried to engage her in conversations about school, what she was doing, and how the other members of the Johnson family were doing. Mary was opening up to him. One night, as they talked, Kurt asked, "How is Little Sammy? He was the first baby I ever held."

"He took his first steps last month. He's doing well. I think it's a fun age. It's too bad you can't see him. I think you would have been big buddies with him."

"How are Sam and Nancy doing?"

"I'm not sure. I think there may be some problems. Nancy is still angry with Sam over losing the store and having to move up here. Nancy and I have gotten close. We certainly agree on that."

"I like Sam, but you can add me to the list with you and Nancy. What about Bob? I feel guilty. Bob tried to help us. I feel like I betrayed him almost as much as I hurt you. I'd like to apologize to him sometime."

"I don't know if he was mad at you or felt bad for me. But you know I've moved on and found someone else to date."

"Yes. I know that. But that doesn't change the fact that I love you and always will. No matter what you do. No matter what happens. I will love you every day of my life until I die. I hope and pray that someday you will once again love me. But I can't control that. Just remember, I will always love you. I take time to pray for you and your family every day, and I'll never stop."

She didn't try to stop him from saying these things. She once again thanked him for the call, which had lasted three hours. *My plan is working!*

It was mid-October. Midterm exams were coming up. Kurt didn't care. Now that he was away from his parents, all the parts of the plan were slowly working out. They worked faster than he had dared to hope. He called Mary on a Wednesday night. She answered, but something was different in her tone.

"Kurt, I won't take any more of your calls. I'm happy with the guy I'm dating. It would be best if you focused on school. Quit calling. Please leave me alone."

They talked for a few more minutes, but nothing changed. This was such a colossal reversal that Kurt just couldn't take it in. *What is happening? This doesn't make sense.*

He lay in bed without sleeping that night. His mind raced. *Was Mrs. Johnson there, bullying her? I can't believe that she likes this guy. I know she loves me. I can't be that wrong. I've never been this sure about anything in my life. I love Mary, and Mary loves me.*

He tried calling a week later, but Mrs. Johnson answered. "Mary doesn't want to talk to you. How many times do I have to tell you? Stop calling her."

The same thing happened the following week. There were still no letters, and now, no phone calls. The only thing going on was a deafening silence. Kurt became discouraged. He would wait a bit and resume his campaign. But it seemed a little different this time. He couldn't see what had changed. He tried sending flowers again, but when he called, Mary was unavailable.

Kurt had brought his car to school when he returned from Thanksgiving. When he finished his last final, he headed home. He debated driving to Indianapolis before going home but wasn't sure what he would say or do when he got there, so he went home.

After he'd been home for a few days, he had a brainstorm. Mary's birthday was only a month away. He went to a small jewelry shop on the square of his hometown and talked to the jeweler there. He was looking for an engagement ring. He still had a little over fifteen hundred dollars available. He was left with twelve hundred if he kept three hundred for bus fare, cab fare, and lodging. The jeweler helped him pick out a ring. Its price was over thirteen, but the jeweler would give it to Kurt for twelve, tax included.

Kurt knew his parents and Mrs. Johnson opposed his relationship with Mary. But the last week of January, she would turn eighteen. Their objections would no longer matter. Her birthday was on a Friday. Kurt had no classes on Fridays next semester. He would arrive in Indianapolis in the early afternoon and try to catch Mary after she got home from school. If the bus schedule didn't allow that, he would arrive on Saturday and meet her in the early afternoon. This plan had to work! Kurt knew that if he knelt before her with an engagement ring, Mary would accept it. He couldn't believe that she did not love him, and faced with that situation, they would be back together forever.

Kurt walked on clouds. He hid the jewelry box in his chest of drawers and started dreaming of what would come. Christmas Day was a nonevent for Kurt. His brother and sister had come home with their families, but he didn't care. He had more important things on his mind. Kurt couldn't wait until Mary's birthday.

The next day, he hiked through some woods with a friend. They gamboled along the top of an icy bluff when Kurt turned around. He thought he'd heard a strange noise. As he turned, he slipped on the ice and went over the bluff headfirst. Fortunately, he didn't land on any boulders, but he landed headfirst on frozen earth after a fall of about sixteen feet. He had a concussion. He spent the next several days lying around the house and taking it easy. Finally, it was all right for him to get out and about again.

Kurt started cruising town in his car. As a matter of habit, he drove by Mary's grandmother's house, only to find several vehicles he recognized there. Mary was probably in town! He drove through Ron's Twirly Top to see if anyone had seen Mary.

Someone said yes. Mary might have been going to the Lucky Dollar.

Kurt took off for the Lucky Dollar. It was a unique place in town. It was just a hangout or clubhouse for the Coffman family. They had seven children, including four boys. The boys built a building behind the house. It was nearly one thousand square feet, one room, no plumbing, but it did have electricity. Kids from all over town would go there to hang out. It was never locked. Sometimes a game of cards would go on, but everyone was always welcome. He'd make things right. Once and for all.

I'm in Love

As Kurt drove over to try to see Mary, his mind raced. *I can finally see her. Talk to her. Look into her eyes and tell her how I feel. Surely this will bring the forgiveness I need. Stir her love for me. This is it.*

Kurt pulled up to the Lucky Dollar. He was still a little dizzy from the concussion. As he parked, he saw Mary's car. His heart skipped a beat. When Kurt entered, Mary saw him and walked out to her car. He followed her. "Mary, may I speak with you?"

"Yes. It's cold out here. Let's get in my car." Mary was behind the steering wheel. Kurt got in on the passenger side and slid toward Mary but not up against her. He felt it was important not to push too hard. A part of him wished he had the ring in his pocket. He could give it to her as a Christmas or New Year's gift.

"How are you doing?"

"Fine."

He looked at her. "You're as beautiful as ever."

But she wasn't smiling.

"I need to tell you how sorry I am for everything. I love you. I want to spend the rest of my life with you. I don't know how I could live without you. Please forgive me."

Mary didn't look at Kurt. Her eyes were straight ahead, as

though she was searching down the road. "You've got to quit calling me. I'm in love with someone else."

He said, or perhaps shouted, "No! You don't mean that. I love you, and you love me. You're just angry with me because I hurt you. Please give me a chance to tell and prove to you how much I love you." He grasped her right arm with his left hand as he said this.

Mary turned and looked at Kurt. The same beautiful brown eyes as ever. Did he see a tear? He wasn't sure. They still seemed to peer into the depths of his soul. But there was no smile, just a thin, straight line where her lips were. "I'm in love with someone else, and I am asking you to promise to quit calling me or writing me." As she said it, she grasped Kurt's left wrist with her left hand, picked it up, and moved it away from her. Mary glanced at his hand as if it were something filthy and disgusting.

Kurt was dizzy, his head reeled, and he couldn't breathe. He looked at her. He couldn't make words come out of his mouth.

"I'm in love with someone else, Kurt. Promise you will not call me or write me anymore."

"I promise," came from his mouth in a hoarse whisper. What else could he say? He sat there as if frozen. *My life is over*.

"Goodbye."

Kurt said, "Goodbye." He exited the car, and she drove out of his life. Kurt stood out in the cold, in six inches of snow, and didn't move for fifteen minutes or more. He was incapable of moving. Someone else left the Lucky Dollar and yelled at Kurt. They told him he was going to freeze to death, standing there without a coat. This awakened Kurt from his stupor.

He got in his car and started driving. Most likely, Kurt drove several laps, cruising around town. He didn't know where he went, what he did, or where he'd been. Eventually, he went home. Everyone was in bed when he got there. Kurt went upstairs to bed. He lay there staring at the ceiling for what seemed a long time. He didn't know. At some point during the night, Kurt fell asleep and didn't wake up until around eleven the next morning.

His mother was in the kitchen when he came downstairs. "Did you have a good time last night?"

His only reply was a few grunts. "Mph. Whew." She said nothing about it, as Kurt was rarely talkative when he first got up. He spent most of his Christmas break in his room reading. On a few occasions, he went out with friends. He didn't talk to anyone. At mealtimes, he hardly touched his food.

He ran one special errand. He took a small package containing a beautiful ring to the jewelry store, where the owner saw him come in.

"Hello Kurt, what do you need?"

Kurt handed the box with the ring back to the jeweler. "May I please return this?"

The jeweler was an older man who liked Kurt. "Of course you can, Kurt. What happened? Or would you rather not talk about it?"

Kurt said hoarsely, with tears in his eyes, "She's in love with someone else."

The owner gave Kurt a refund and patted him on the back. "There will be better days ahead. You're a fine young man. Just hang in there."

Kurt nodded, thanked him, and went back home. He wanted to go to school now to be an invisible face among thirty thousand students again. To disappear. He didn't want anyone to ask him about Mary. To see anything that would remind him of Mary.

As Kurt headed back to school, the only thing he knew for sure was that his life would never be the same. Not only would it never be the same, but it felt as though it would not be worth living. Getting out of bed to face the new day each morning was difficult. Kurt felt like he was living in a horrible dream and prayed that he would someday awaken and all of this would go away.

Stumbling through the Dark

The days ahead were difficult for Kurt. He was no longer interested in school. Or anything. Anyone knowledgeable would have seen that he was suffering from severe depression. He went through his days as an unthinking, dumb beast. He slept, ate, and attended classes. Kurt did not socialize with anyone. His parents wondered why he no longer called or wrote home regularly. They didn't realize he had given up on life.

Mary's birthday came and went. Kurt's plans tormented him on that day. He went to the student union, found a quiet nook, and sat there. He didn't read. Didn't listen to music or any other entertainment. Kurt just watched people as they came and went. Some were happy, others serious, and some foolish. The world was moving on. The job for him was to keep trying to find some meaning and value in his life, even if it felt as though it was over and no longer worth living. There was a realization that his judgment was very flawed at the moment, and he should not make any major decisions. His hopes and his spirit had been crushed.

It would take time to heal, and he must give himself time to heal. He was taking one day at a time and attempting to try. This wasn't much of a plan; it was not even a good plan, but it was the best he could do for now. Kurt walked to his dorm room and lay in bed until he finally fell asleep.

Classes kept Kurt busy part of the time. It had been years since he'd studied, even though he made good grades. But he would do anything to keep busy. If he was busy, he didn't think about Mary—his brilliant move in scheduling classes so that he had Fridays free returned to haunt him. There wasn't going to be any taking the bus to Indianapolis now. Friday was just a day to think about what might have been.

Valentine's Day came around. There was a floor party at his dorm that night, which was a Saturday. Kurt's roommate was tending the bar at the party. The only drink Kurt had ever had was a sip of wine at Bob Johnson's house when he had been with Mary the previous Christmas. Depressed, lonely, and confused, Kurt decided to try a drink. Unbeknownst to him, his roommate talked to the other bartenders. If Kurt asked for anything, he would prepare the drink. He understood Kurt didn't drink and made every drink a double or triple. After a few drinks, Kurt was drunk.

At first he didn't realize it. He noticed he was talking more than he ever had in his life. His filters didn't work. Kurt was being very rude and obnoxious. He walked up to people and butted in on conversations. He made several loud, sarcastic remarks to a couple having a private conversation. "You only think you're having a good time! You'll be sorry! If you make one little mistake, she'll kick you out!" He went on and on.

They'd had enough. "Why don't you take a walk."

"I don't want to go for a walk. It's cold outside."

"You need to go for a long walk."

"Who are you to tell me I need to take a walk?"

They had to leave to get away from him. If someone was having a good time, it made Kurt angry.

He went up to a group of people who were laughing at a joke. "You guys are being too loud! You need to leave!"

"Kurt, just shut up and go away."

"It's you that needs to shut up and go away! That joke wasn't even funny! Just stop it!"

A friend approached him and said, "Hey Kurt, I don't think you realize it, but you're drunk. You probably need to go somewhere quiet and calm down."

After that, Kurt returned to his room, lay on his bed, and

cried. Some of this was due to missing Mary, and some of it was due to feeling guilty over getting drunk. The bed seemed to spin, but Kurt rolled over and clutched the sides of the bed to hang on. His stomach felt a little queasy. He dropped off into a deep sleep. When he awakened the following day, there was no hangover.

That was the second and last time Kurt ever had a drink. He hated the person he became that night. It was embarrassing to see some of the people he'd talked to that night in the days following the party. As he remembered bits and pieces of conversation, it was clear he'd been pretty overbearing with several people. There were others with whom he had been a weepy, whiny boor.

In the future, Kurt would be careful about his behavior and try very hard to focus on his schoolwork. Two of his classes were interesting, and he focused on them. The others were not at all what he had hoped for, and though he did the necessary work, he did not give them the same level of effort. The days slowly passed, and spring break arrived.

While he was home on spring break, he got in touch with several of his old friends. It was warmer there, allowing him to play quite a bit of tennis. He also spent several days hiking through nearby woodlands. One day, he went to a bluff and creek where his ancestors had settled nearly one hundred fifty years ago. It was one of his favorite places. Walking in the shadows of his ancestors seemed to give him a peace he hadn't known in quite some time.

The day before he headed back to school, Kurt's father said, "Kurt, your mother and I need to talk to you." He wondered if it would be about Mary. It was not. They sat at the kitchen table. His father began the conversation. "You need to know that our family is about to have a major change. The franchisor for our store is changing its business model. For me to stay in business, your mother and I would have to go more than half a million dollars in debt. At our age, the risk is foolish. I'm turning sixty this year. I wasn't planning on retiring until you graduated from school. But they've offered me an early out that I can take on my birthday this year. They will find someone else to purchase the franchise."

His mother cut in. "You won't be able to go back to the university next year. We can't afford it. We would be willing to borrow the money if you want to cosign the loan and run the store. It would be yours. Your father and I would gladly help you until you are comfortable."

"I appreciate the offer, but I don't want to run the store the rest of my life. Could you fill out a financial aid form so I could take out a few loans and finance my education?"

"We aren't going to fill one of those out. They never did any good for your brother and won't do you any good."

"I guess the discussion is over. I hope you enjoy your retirement, Dad."

Kurt pondered these things on the train back to school. Would returning home be better than returning to school? While he was at school, his life seemed to fall apart. On the other hand, the beginning and end of his relationship with Mary both occurred at home. He realized that she would haunt his thoughts wherever he went. There was nothing to be done but do his best wherever he happened to be. Hard work was the best thing to do.

The remainder of the semester was difficult, but Kurt did well in his classes. His social life was nonexistent, but he didn't want one. The truth was that Kurt was in mourning. It was as if the love of his life had died. With her passing, a part of Kurt himself died. He plodded through life, trying to survive.

On his last day at the university, the professor in his history class wanted to speak with him. Kurt stopped by with no idea what to expect. He entered the office and sat down.

"Kurt, what is your major?"

"Accounting."

Dr. Darcy looked disappointed. "How are you doing in accounting?"

"Reasonably well. I don't care for it. Why?"

"Because I've never had a student as able as you in an under-graduate history course. I hoped that you were going to major in history. But I realize that is not a popular decision these days."

"I love history. It and theology are the two subjects I love most. My guidance counselors always told me they were dead-ends. Pursue a degree in accounting or engineering. I knew I would hate engineering, so accounting seemed the way to go. The truth is, I believe being an accountant would bore me to death."

"Well, should you ever decide you want to attend graduate school in history, I would be happy to provide a letter of recom-mendation. Despite currently prevailing opinions, there are careers available for historians. I believe you could do very well for yourself in that field."

I can't believe this is happening. I'd love this. But I'm not coming back. I may as well tell him it won't work. I hate my life.

"Sir," came the answer, "I can't tell you how much I appre-ciate your offer. There is a problem though. My father was forced to retire early a few weeks ago, and I won't be able to return to the university next year."

"If you continue your education elsewhere, the offer will still be there when you graduate. I've enjoyed having you in my class."

For the first time in months, Kurt had good news about something.

"Thank you, Professor Darcy. I will. Thank you more than I can ever express."

"Well, we've got that settled. I suppose you are anxious to get home for summer break. Good luck to you. I'll be waiting to hear from you." Dr. Darcy stood.

"Goodbye. Thank you again."

He walked out of the office and returned to his dorm. His parents would be there to pick him up the next day. The offer from Dr. Darcy was the kindest thing anyone had done for Kurt in quite some time. The thought of accounting and engineering made him ill. Going to graduate school in history sounded like a dream come true. Finally, something had gone right.

Chapter 11
Regrouping

Intentional Exhaustion

That summer, Kurt got a job at a local grocery store. Even though he had left school happier than he'd been in five months, he still suffered from depression. After enrolling at a nearby community college for the fall, Kurt had his future planned for the following year. He aimed to save enough money to pay for his final two years of college.

Kurt kept a journal. When he couldn't sleep at night, it seemed to help to put his rambling thoughts on paper. Sometimes his writing was rational and coherent. At other times, it was frenzied. Sometimes it was insightful; other times, it was a despairing lamentation. But it did help him get to sleep.

Over the summer, his friends set him up for double dates. Kurt did go, but primarily to spend time with his friends. He wound up dating one girl for several months. When Kurt realized the girl was getting somewhat serious about their relationship, he broke up with her. The truth was, he was still in love with Mary. It was wrong to lead anyone on or allow them to expect more than just an occasional date.

Kurt took eighteen hours per semester and worked forty-two hours weekly at the grocery store. Every free night, he was out with his friends. Kurt still had a lot of anger to work out regarding his parents. For two semesters, Kurt averaged about five hours of sleep per night. About once every five or six weeks, Kurt would come home from work on Friday night and go straight to bed. After working all day on Saturday, he would again come home and go to bed. Sunday, after getting home from church, he would do the same. He would be so exhausted that he slept for nearly forty hours over three days. Then he would go back to the busy routine again.

Kurt rarely went out with a girl more than once at this point. He came home around midnight, even on weeknights. One evening, he saw an acquaintance four years older out cruising. They stopped to talk for a few minutes. Chuck Davis had met Kurt while Kurt worked at his father's hardware store. Over the years, they bumped into one another. Chuck was waiting for a friend who was working at a factory. He got back to town around midnight. Kurt decided to hang out with Chuck.

Chuck was around five feet ten inches tall, with short, curly, light brown hair. He had an aquiline nose, blue eyes, and a firm chin. Chuck was very muscular. He ran at least two miles daily, lifted weights, and kept himself in great shape.

Chuck had two close friends, Ronnie and Simon. Simon worked at a factory. Ronnie attended a nearby university with Chuck. Ronnie and Simon were two years older than Kurt. The four of them began to hang out together quite a bit, particularly on weekends. During the week, Ronnie and Chuck were away at school. When they were all in town, they were inseparable. Kurt didn't see as much of his old friends, other than Roger Sloan. His other friends were just a painful reminder of all that had passed.

Kurt continued driving by Mary's old home and her grand-mother's on his nightly prowls. He didn't know what he would do if anyone ever turned up, but a part of him still believed Mary loved him. The words she spoke at their parting were deliberately designed to hurt him. When he considered the situation from Mary's point of view, he understood that.

She saw the shock and pain that hit him when she told him she was in love with someone else. The dagger had gone straight to his heart. She had her revenge. Who could blame her? Kurt didn't. He understood. But he had no more ideas on how to let her know. The promise she dragged out of him came back to haunt him again and again. He continued to drive by the two places he thought she might turn up, hoping that something would happen, although he didn't know what.

In the spring, Kurt, Chuck, Ronnie, and Simon started dating four girls in town who were all friends. The eight of them were all friends. Again, Kurt dated someone to hang out with his friends. It was another meaningless relationship.

The four couples met at a local burger place on their first date. They sat, talked, and ate. Simon played the jukebox several times. Kurt was with a girl named Meghan McGill. They'd never met before. She was very quiet. An introvert. She was naive and failed to get the jokes the others told. None of this bothered Kurt. The louder members of the party got on his nerves. After they finished, each couple left separately.

Kurt and Meghan cruised around town. It was difficult for Kurt to find things to talk about. Meghan didn't seem passionate about anything. She talked about school. She did like some of the music played on his car stereo. They sang along with a few of the songs. Meghan had a beautiful singing voice. When Kurt felt they had been gone a respectable amount of time, he took her home and walked her to the door. They kissed good night. Kurt went home. He was tired and went to bed.

A Series of Surprises

Kurt received a package in the mail one day that shocked him. When he looked at the return address, his jaw dropped. It was from Mrs. Johnson. His hands trembled as he opened it. The package contained the last of Kurt's possessions that had been given to Mary. There was a friendly note inside.

Dear Kurt,

I was cleaning out Mary's old room and found these. It seemed only right to return them to you. Mary got married and moved out last spring. I realize now that you were a nice boy. I'm sorry that things didn't work out between you and Mary. My very best wishes to you.

Sincerely,
Stella Johnson

Mary fell in love during her senior year, graduated, and started college. But in the spring of her freshman year, Mary got married. Kurt didn't want to believe it. Why would Mrs. Johnson say she wished it had worked out? She said he was a nice boy. Something wasn't right. He knew of no way to find out the truth of the matter. He again plunged into a period of gloom.

Everyone told Kurt that Meghan, the girl he'd gone out with two or three times, was perfect for him. He needed to get over Mary and take this girl out. Kurt was not interested in her, and everyone telling him what to do annoyed him. Part of the mess in his life was because everyone else seemed to think they knew what was best for Kurt, and he was sick of it. He was getting ready to find someone else to date.

One evening, the eight of them went out again. Kurt thought it would be his last date with Meghan. For some reason, she was wound up that night. They went to a terrible movie. On the way home, Chuck decided to take back roads instead of the highway. They came to the end of the paved road. Whichever direction they continued would be a gravel road. They stopped to discuss which way to go.

"Chuck, you're going to get us lost! You don't have any idea where you are. We need to turn around and get on the highway."

"Meghan, Chuck knows these roads. You need to calm down."

"It's been a while since I've been through here. I need to go straight, but I'm not sure. Why don't you pick a direction? We'll go that way, Meghan."

"I think it's a big mistake, but since you thought we should go straight, let's go straight."

The road had several curves and came to a tee. "Which way should we go, Meghan? I'm leaving it up to you to decide."

"I don't know. I think we're lost. Why don't we turn around?"

"How about if I flip a coin? Heads left, tails right," Kurt suggested. Chuck knew these roads like the back of his hand. Kurt had often gone down them with him.

"Okay, flip a coin, Kurt."

"Heads. Turn left."

"This is crazy. We're going to get lost."

This continued for a while. Meghan was convinced they were hopelessly lost. Chuck made a suggestion. "Meghan, why don't we pull in at the next house we come to? You can go to the door and ask for directions. Kurt can go to the door with you."

"I don't know. Will you come with me, Kurt?"

"Sure. I'd be happy to."

They came to a house and slowed down. "I've changed my mind. I can't go to the door. I'd feel foolish. They won't know who I am, which would be embarrassing."

"If that's how you want it, we'll keep driving. Here's a place where we can go straight or turn left. What do you think?"

"I can flip a coin again. It's heads. Turn left." After they'd gone a little way down the road, they saw some headlights approaching. "Chuck, why don't you slow down and see if we can get this car to stop? I'll get out and ask them for directions."

"What? Oh, sure. I'll try to get them to stop." He slowed down. The other car slowed down but couldn't stop until it passed them. Kurt hopped out and went to the other vehicle.

"Hi, Jack. Don't talk too loudly. We've got a girl convinced we're lost. I'm supposed to be getting directions. She thinks we're close to Pickle City. What should I say?"

"Go straight for two miles, and the road will be paved. Then it will take you straight into Pickle City."

Kurt hurried back to the car and gave Chuck the directions. "I knew it! I told you guys you were lost. But you wouldn't listen! See! I was right. I said we were close to Pickle City!"

They followed the road until it turned back into a paved road. "See. We never should have gone this way! You should have listened to me."

A few minutes later, they came to a highway. Everyone looked at the highway, and someone said, "Hey! We're only a mile from town. We're nowhere near Pickle City. We're home."

Everyone burst out laughing, but no one harder than Meghan. "You guys knew! You knew all along. You were playing a joke on me."

"We ought to tell you a couple of things. The house where we tried to get you to ask for directions was Chuck's. When that didn't work, we managed to stop his brother Jack on the way home from a date. That's where I got my directions." Kurt started laughing and was delighted that Meghan laughed too.

Meghan was the life of the party. He was having fun on a date for the first time since he'd gone out with Mary.

The next week, all his friends told him they were sorry

because they had been wrong about Meghan. As silly as she had acted the previous Saturday night, it was obvious that she was a bad match for someone as serious as Kurt. Telling Kurt what to do was like waving a red flag in front of a bull. Kurt decided to hold off deciding. He knew he wasn't thinking straight, between forty-two hours at work, eighteen hours in course load at school, running on five hours of sleep each night, and the news that Mary had married someone else. Kurt just needed everyone to back off.

One afternoon, Kurt cruised with Roger Sloan. He saw Mary parked in a car along the cruise route. His stomach flipped. "Roger, take me back to my car. I need to see Mary. I think she wants to tell me something. I'd rather be alone when I talk to her."

Roger headed toward Kurt's car. "Okay. Let's turn here. It'll be faster."

Is Mary waiting to tell me she's married? Maybe tell me that she loves me; show me a big diamond ring and tell me how wonderful her husband is. Anyway, I've got to know. It was a combination of hope and torture.

On the shortcut, Roger's car got stuck in the mud. It took them fifteen or twenty minutes to get out of it. When Kurt arrived at his car, he drove to where Mary had been parked. She was gone. He went by the house and by her grandmother's. No one was at either place. He cruised the rest of the night, but there was no sign of Mary. Whatever it was, he had missed his opportunity to speak to her.

Between the long hours at the store, a maximum load at school, and running around late into the night with his friends, Kurt was exhausted. He kept telling himself this dulled the emotional pain. Most of the time, when Kurt was driving and was alone, he pushed his car to the max, driving eighty to ninety miles per hour.

One day he was running late on the way to school and

decided to take a shortcut. There was a gravel road that veered off from the highway and would save three or four miles. Kurt hit the gravel at well over eighty miles per hour. The next thing he knew, the car spun around until it stopped in the ditch a quarter mile down the road. Kurt had been thrown around inside the car but felt all right. His heart was racing. He was a little shaky, but he wasn't injured.

While the car had been out of control, it was as though he wasn't in it. He was looking down at it from the roof of the car. It was a calm, almost peaceful feeling. After the car came to a stop, he was back to himself again. When he got out to look at the car, he saw the passenger side front tire was ripped to shreds. He didn't know if it was a blowout that caused the accident or the accident that destroyed the tire. After fixing the tire, he turned around and drove to Chuck's house. He knew Chuck was home for spring break. The two of them went for a hike that day. It was the first time he'd relaxed in a long time.

Kurt and Chuck had decided to room together at school the following year. They considered different schools. Kurt had intended to return to Illinois but wasn't sure he could stand some of the memories attached to that place. Chuck was interested in Illinois State, in Bloomington. They agreed to try Illinois State. Both were accepted and got housing together.

With the immediate future sorted out, Kurt and Chuck enjoyed getting out and hiking through the Shawnee National Forest. When they both had free days, they would search for waterfalls, natural bridges, swimming holes, and unusual rock formations. During their hikes, they would discuss their love lives. Kurt shared with Chuck many of the things that had happened with Mary. He told Chuck he was messed up. It was nice to have one person in the world he could tell all that had happened.

Kurt's friend Tracker came by one day with a new motorcycle. He was going on a ride with some friends to Indianapolis.

Tracker asked if Kurt could give him Mary's address so that he could stop in and see her. Kurt was more than happy to provide both her address and telephone number. He wondered how Mary would treat Tracker but hoped he would find out some news when Tracker got home.

Three days later, Tracker stopped to visit Kurt. "Why didn't you tell me Mary was married?"

"Is she? I'd heard something but wasn't sure."

"I knocked on the door, and her mom came to the door. I asked if Mary was home. She said Mary had married some guy from Indianapolis. I can't remember the name she gave me, but anyway, she said Mary didn't live there anymore."

Kurt talked with Tracker a bit longer, but another part of him died, down deep. *I guess it must be true. I guess it's over.* Still, he loved her, and he continued to feel that deep inside, she loved him too.

The weekend before he and Chuck headed to school, they were hanging out at Ron's Twirly Top. A familiar car was there. It was Lori and Terry. When Lori saw Kurt, she walked up to him. "Hey, Terry! Here's another one of Mary's ex-boyfriends!" Turning to face Kurt, she said, "You should have come to her wedding. It was nice. The guy she married is loaded with money and made the rest of you guys look bad. It's the first time I've seen her happy." Then Lori turned and walked off.

Running Away

"Let's get out of here." They took off.

"She enjoyed rubbing that in my face. Mary's mother told me. She told Tracker. Lori told me. Terry didn't deny it. I guess it's true. Mary got married."

"Do you want to talk about it, Kurt?"

"No. Let's find something to take my mind off it." They

drove around out in the country for a while. Then Kurt went home.

They both arrived in Bloomington a few days later. There weren't any problems as they got through the opening week of school. But Kurt hated his classes. Hated his instructors. Kurt hated pretty much everyone and everything. He could not accept the double confirmation of Mary's wedding and marriage. Yet there it was. It had happened, and he was helpless to do anything about it. He supposed Mary had fallen in love with this other guy. Maybe he had lived believing a fairy tale for the last three years.

He checked with the bursar's office and discovered he could receive a full refund for tuition and fees if he dropped out before the end of the second week of classes. Without discussing it with anyone, he dropped out. He spent a few days with Chuck and figured he needed to go home and find a job. They found someone to sublet Kurt's room. With that, Kurt headed back home.

A few weeks later, Chuck was back in town. The next semester, Chuck went back to the school Ronnie was attending. Meanwhile, Kurt tried to find a job. He had no interest in going back to school. His parents seemed relieved that he was not attending school and living at home. He got a teller position at a local bank.

Kurt had a few more accidents in his car over the next six months. They were always at high speed on bad roads. He went to a therapist who suggested he was attempting to commit suicide by wrecking his car. There was a ring of truth in what she said. Based on his religious beliefs, Kurt realized he needed to slow down and find a different way to deal with stress and his sense of failure.

The bank was not a career path he would have chosen, but it was very much a low-stress position, which was quite a relief after two years of overworking himself to exhaustion. Because he lived with his parents, he could save some money, even though the pay was not great. During this period, he continued to date Meghan.

Sometimes his thoughts would turn to Mary when he was with Meghan. He would not hear what was being said. His eyes would lose their focus as he stared off into the distance. Meghan's voice would jolt him back to reality. She would ask what was on his mind. Kurt always said, "Nothing." He claimed that sometimes he just zoned out.

It was true. No one knew that the place he went to was with Mary. He pictured her in his mind, thinking about her voice, smile, and piercing brown eyes. Most of all, it was a place where he was holding Mary's hand, looking into those eyes, and seeing that special smile.

Kurt felt like life was passing him by. He had no sense of direction or purpose. Knowing that Mary had a husband just didn't seem real. Yet it was true. He went over and over in his head the times he had failed her. He kept rethinking what he should or could have done.

Someone else had married Mary. She loved someone else. Because of his failures, she had moved on. He needed to do the same. But then he would be driving down the road and remember the night he almost wrecked his car because he was looking at her in all her beauty and sweetness. He could imagine the feel of her head resting on his shoulder and her hand in his. There seemed to be no escape. What was he to do? Kurt had no idea.

It was like he was walking through the woods on a cloudy night. He couldn't see where he was going. He stumbled along the best he could. That was his life, stumbling through the dark.

Chapter 12
Getting On With Life

Desperate Decision

Time passed, although for Kurt, it didn't fly. It was more of a slow, steady drumbeat. Three years had passed since he hoarsely whispered his promise to Mary. Every day, he mentioned Mary in his prayers. He tried to pray for her husband, whoever he might be, but there were days he couldn't bear to do that. Work was going well enough, but it wasn't anything he was passionate about. He had settled into a steady routine of dating Meghan. Life wasn't great, but it was less unbearable than it had been three years ago.

Kurt's circle of close friends had gotten smaller over the years. Ronnie married and ran in a different circle. Racket and Simon moved in together and started doing drugs. Rudy had just disappeared. The only two friends that Kurt saw regularly were Roger Sloan and Chuck Davis.

Mary had rejected him and married someone else. In a long period of depression, Kurt had been nearly suicidal for a while. His mental health had finally improved. He'd given up on his dream of a degree in history but had a decent job, working his way up at the bank. Mary had been married for over two years.

One afternoon on a hike, Kurt asked Chuck for advice. "Do you think two people who are good friends could make marriage work?"

"I'm not sure. Give me more information."

"They like one another. Have a lot of common interests. Not a lot of romantic feelings. What do you think?"

"If they committed to it, yes. Isn't that how arranged marriages worked?"

"I guess you're right. It would be a lot like an arranged marriage." They discussed it for the rest of the afternoon.

It was time for Kurt to move on with his life. He couldn't wait around for another man's wife. As the days crawled by, Mary's third anniversary was approaching. Kurt saw Lori and Terry in town once again. Lori again taunted him with news about how happily married Kurt's ex (Mary) was. She seemed to delight in calling Kurt "Mary's ex" and calling Mary "Kurt's ex." His decision was made.

A few months later, Kurt was at Meghan's house. They were alone in the kitchen. Without any lead-up, Kurt asked, "So, would you like to get married? We could pick out a ring next week."

"Okay. When?"

"We could pick the ring next Wednesday. I have a doctor's appointment and have the afternoon off."

"Yes. I can do that."

It wasn't romantic. They were two decent people who had fun together. On Wednesday they bought the ring and showed it to their families. The wedding was set for a few months later.

The wedding seemed to come rapidly. Meghan's mother made most of the decisions about the wedding, even choosing the maid of honor and bridesmaids. She complained that she did not receive enough notice of the engagement to plan properly. For the first time in years, time did not drag.

Kurt's last act before going to the wedding was to destroy the journal he had been keeping. It was full of the ramblings of someone who was in a deep state of depression. It apologized for his behavior in case of his unexpected death. He wrote page after page about how much he loved Mary, missed Mary, and felt as though he couldn't live without her. *These weren't meant for anyone to see unless I was dead. I think they were a suicide note.* He was doing his best to build a new life. His old life had ended the day he was told Mary had married someone else.

After their honeymoon, Kurt and Meghan settled down and began a normal life together. He was doing well at the bank, and Meghan worked part-time as an office clerk. Her family did not attend church, but Meghan had attended the same church as Kurt off and on while growing up.

Kurt's parents loved Meghan, and she was also very close to them. One day, as Kurt and his father talked, Mr. Kellerman said, "Kurt, that girl is crazy about you. Meghan is the girl for you."

This seemed to Kurt to be a strange comment. As he pondered it, Kurt realized his father was attempting to justify his hostility to Mary. The effect on Kurt was the opposite of what his father intended. A few days later, Kurt asked his father, "Were you trying to say something about Mary the other day?"

"No. I was just talking about how good a match Meghan is for you."

"So you were saying Meghan is a better match for me than Mary was?"

"Well, I wasn't saying that, but now that you mention it, yes. Mary was a Catholic, her parents were divorced, and she wasn't our kind of people."

Kurt exploded. His face turned red. Heart racing, he flapped his arms in the air. His entire body was shaking. "Her parents were not divorced! Mary's dad was a farmer who was killed in a farming accident. She loved you and Mom. She thought—no, we thought you both liked her. I can't believe you said that!"

Kurt stormed off. He didn't know what to do. This conversation stirred up all sorts of emotions deep within. It also brought back all kinds of memories that constantly simmered just below the surface. He had further confirmation that his parents had opposed his relationship with Mary. At the same time, Meghan was his wife. Kurt had a very high view of marriage. He would never leave Meghan. Besides, Mary was the wife of someone else. But it filled Kurt with bitterness to know his parents' thoughts on the situation.

To top it all off, something was always happening to bring his thoughts back to Mary. Even when he could get his mind off her for a few minutes, someone else would bring her up to Kurt. Anyone who had known Kurt before or while he was dating Mary could see that he had never gotten over their breakup. Even in his happiest moments, a sense of sadness hung over him like a cloud.

Putting a Life Back Together

Kurt tried to get back on track with his life. He needed to keep his focus and not live in the past. Work was going well, and Kurt moved from a teller position to a loan officer. One day, Meghan wasn't around when he got home from work. She'd had a doctor's appointment and was running a bit late. Kurt didn't think anything of it and went ahead with some work around the house. A few minutes later, Meghan pulled into the drive. Kurt met her at the door. Meghan smiled from ear to ear.

Kurt asked, "What's going on?"

"I'm expecting!"

"That's wonderful!" He was happier in that moment than he'd been in years. The couple came together in a long, warm embrace. They were both overjoyed. That night, they went out for dinner to celebrate. They intended not to announce it for a while, but Meghan began to have severe morning sickness. She was often unable to go to work.

They went to Meghan's parents to announce it. Her parents were happy to anticipate their first grandchild but wanted to know why they hadn't been told earlier. (This was to become a theme with them.) After telling Meghan's parents, they went to Kurt's parents' home.

Mrs. Kellerman was on the telephone, talking to Kurt's sister. He tried to wait, but the call dragged on for another thirty minutes. Finally, his mother asked if Kurt had anything to tell his sister. He responded, "Ask her how she would like a new niece or nephew."

Mrs. Kellerman repeated the question. He could hear his sister yell over the phone, "Really?!"

Kurt's mother looked confused, and then a look of comprehension descended over her face. She dropped the receiver, ran across the room to Meghan, and hugged her. Kurt's sister's voice came from the phone, rather loud and confused. He picked it up and explained things to her. She congratulated Kurt. Then they hung up.

The next several months went by fast. Meghan was one of those women who glowed when she was expecting. She carried the baby high and right in front. She did not have the frumpy, miserable look some women have during pregnancy. Once the morning sickness had passed, she smiled almost nonstop until the pregnancy was over.

Kurt was working in the yard when Meghan called out to him—the time had come. They drove to the hospital. After a long, hard labor, the Kellermans had a baby boy. They named him John Adam Kellerman. He was large, at ten pounds. He had blue eyes, like his father. He had his mother's dark hair and nose. Kurt claimed he had large feet. They were thrilled with their son.

Friends and family members visited their small apartment to see the new child. Meghan recovered quickly. She talked to John, read to John, and most of all, sang to John. John was bright and intelligent. Kurt was always willing to help with the baby when he got home from the bank.

As Meghan and Kurt adjusted to life as a family of three, a few changes occurred at work. The president had asked Kurt to work as a loan officer in one of the bank's smaller branches. It was a local bank that was trying to expand to include a fair amount of southern and central Illinois. It focused on small towns and farming communities.

Kurt had a great-uncle, Robert Turner, who'd been a successful man of business. Kurt sought advice from him. "I didn't finish college. What do I need to succeed in business?"

"The key to success is to sell yourself. Never refuse to do an honest job, whether it's something you want to do or not. This will lead to greater responsibilities. To better situations."

This is how you impress your boss and persuade him to give you better opportunities. Kurt went to the tiny, out-of-the-way location to work as a loan officer.

Kurt enjoyed the branch office. After he'd been there around six months, one day the manager complained about some issues with how he felt. While he was out to lunch, someone called the bank and said the manager had suffered a heart attack. Kurt called the main office to see what needed to be done. They asked if he could manage the branch for a few days until someone came to check out the situation.

A week later, a board member who had retired from the bank dropped by. His name was Art Kessler. He spent the day looking things over and asked Kurt numerous questions. After leaving, Kurt had no idea what to expect. He got a call that the current branch manager wouldn't be back for at least three months. Two days later, the bank president came by to meet with Kurt.

"I talked to Art Kessler. He recommended we ask you to manage the branch until Joe returns. I agreed. We would pay you the salary of a branch manager during that period. When Joe returns, you would go back to a loan officer in duties and salary. What do you think?"

"Thank you, sir. I'd be happy to do it."

"That's great. If you need any help, call me or Art."

Three months stretched into four, and Kurt enjoyed the additional duties. He was putting in longer hours but liked the challenges involved. Kurt began thinking he would like to find a branch manager position instead of being a loan officer. Art suggested Kurt pursue additional education in a few banking-related areas, primarily business administration courses. It was a bit of a strain between work and the baby, but Kurt did it.

A year later, a branch manager position came open in a town about forty miles away. Kurt was able to get the position. This required moving to a new community. Meghan and Kurt found a house in the new town, purchased it, and settled. It was good for them to be further away from their parents. In the new community, they found a church they both liked, made several new friends with people their age, and came to rely on one another.

Maybe living in a new community with Meghan and John and attending a new church will finally help me move on with my life. There wouldn't be as many reminders of Mary. This was it. He could have peace of mind.

Meghan had a second son shortly after moving. He was named James Robert Kellerman. She and Kurt were thrilled to have a second child. Meghan enjoyed getting together with other stay-at-home mothers and doing activities together. Kurt enjoyed making new friends at their church and being the branch manager. Kurt and Meghan were happy.

Still, Mary was there. In the back roads of his mind, she reappeared. Kurt felt guilty for remembering her and thinking about her, but most of all for feeling he still loved her. After all, Meghan was a faithful wife and had given him two sons. He should be happy. He needed to get Mary out of his mind.

Successes

Kurt had the bank sponsor some children's league teams as time passed. He coached the baseball teams himself. John and James had Kurt as a coach at times. The entire family had a great time at these events. Many of their friends were at the games and had children on Kurt's teams.

The church the Kellermans attended ordained Kurt as a deacon. This involved a lot of volunteer work visiting those who were sick, had a death in the family, or had financial or other needs. He found this work to be very rewarding. It provided him with a sense of purpose and joy.

Once again, Meghan expected a child. This time, she had a baby girl. They chose the name Jennifer Leigh. Kurt was almost afraid to hold her. She was much smaller than either of the boys had been at birth. Everyone in the family was delighted to have a baby girl.

Kurt was thrilled to have three healthy children. When he got home from work, Kurt would roughhouse with the boys, rock his daughter, and enjoy quiet evenings with his family. Meghan was a good mother. She disliked attending some of the social functions necessary for a branch manager and his wife. She preferred to be home with her children or together as a family. Still, she tried to support Kurt in his career.

Even though he and Meghan had achieved a degree of happiness together, Mary still haunted him day and night. He dreamed about her. When he drove, he would see Mary sitting in the car smiling and those beautiful brown eyes looking at him. Every day it seemed there were dozens of little reminders of Mary. Because his thoughts ran to Mary, Kurt questioned whether he was being faithful to Meghan. He felt guilty for marrying Meghan while still being in love with Mary.

He tried to get her out of his head, but it seemed impossible. He went to a psychologist without telling anyone, hoping he could work through it. Therapy didn't help. Even though Kurt loved Meghan, it was not a passionate, romantic love. She was a good mother, faithful wife, excellent homemaker, and friend. She had helped him through some tough times to rebuild his life.

This caused Kurt even more anxiety and guilt. Kurt would never divorce Meghan unless she cheated on him. His moral compass came from the Bible and the teachings of the church. It was his sense of faithfulness to God that guided him through life. He had a problem.

The second issue in Kurt's life was his job. He enjoyed the work. He liked the people at his branch. But there had been a few surprises for him after he became a branch manager. After about two years, the bank was bought out by a larger regional bank. Kurt was able to keep his position. But now there was a change in the corporate atmosphere.

The new president, Jimmy Goodwin, held all the branch manager meetings at hotel bars. Spouses were not allowed at the overnight meetings, which were a mixture of drinking and carousing. While there were discussions of business and some training, Jimmy encouraged affairs among the managers. Over time, it became evident that Goodwin wanted to get things on his people to hold over their heads.

Kurt detested these meetings. At the first meeting, he talked to another manager, Frankie Evans, whom he trusted. The two of them debated what was going on. Kurt said, "I can't work here much longer. My career is over."

A little while later, a manager from one of the company's

banks approached Kurt with two drinks in her hands. She was tall and thin, with bleached blond hair that grew to just above her shoulders. Her face was oval with pale gray eyes, flared nostrils, and long, dangling earrings. Kurt thought she was probably around his age but looked older because of some wild living. She held one drink out for Kurt. "My name is Helen Jones. Who are you?"

"You can call me Wally Cleaver. (Wally Cleaver was a character in the sitcom *Leave It to Beaver*. He portrayed the clean-cut, All-American boy.) I'm a good boy and should stay away from girls like you." He smiled as he said this and added, "By the way, thank you for the offer, but I don't drink either."

Helen looked stunned. "You couldn't handle me if your life depended on it."

"That's probably why I'm supposed to stay away from girls like you."

Everyone laughed at this, including Helen. Jimmy Goodwin stood right there. He took it all in. Kurt was not going to be one of "his guys." Kurt would not be seeing any promotions. Any raises would be the minimum necessary within the payroll system.

Kurt looked at Frankie. He'd seen everything as it took place. Frankie looked scared. A little later, Kurt saw Frankie out on the dance floor with Helen. When he got a chance, Kurt asked Frankie what he was doing. Frankie said, "I'll go along with them on the little stuff. I'll drink, dance, and swap jokes at the bar to show I'm a regular guy. I won't cheat on my wife."

"If you go at it that way, they'll think you've double-crossed them and make life hard on you at some point. If you stop it right from the beginning, you'll never see any promotions, but you've established that you won't play their games."

"I've got this. I know what I'm doing and what I won't do. I'll still get promoted. I'm not going to be dead in the water like you."

Kurt hoped, rather than believed, Frankie was right. Kurt deliberated other options for his career. Each meeting was just more of the same. Kurt was correct; they just ignored him and left him alone. He wasn't their guy. He was happy to get free Cokes as the designated driver at every meeting. Three or four other managers had taken a similar approach to Kurt. That little group always stayed around one another for support and safety at the meetings. Frankie slipped further and further away.

Meghan wanted to know what went on at these meetings. Kurt figured it was best to tell her the truth and how he had responded. She was upset at first, but she trusted Kurt.

"Are you sure being so blunt won't cause problems?"

"I had to make it clear that I wouldn't play their game. They would think I was okay with it if I hadn't been so blunt. You are right though. My days at the bank are numbered. I need to find something else."

"Why?"

"I'm not willing to drink and sleep around. Eventually, Mr. Goodwin will get tired of putting up with me."

Life Goes On

Kurt continued to work hard but no longer enjoyed it as he once had. He was popular in the office and the community but not with corporate headquarters. He was able to reduce expenses regularly while increasing deposits and generating loans. During the manager meetings, his numbers were in the top five, although not necessarily at number one. At one meeting, Art Kessler made a presentation. He pointed to Kurt. "Look at this graph of Kellerman's numbers. He's always among the top five. He's never below that. He is rarely, if ever, number one, but it is difficult to be number one consistently. You need to lead your branch the way Kellerman does."

Jimmy Goodwin's face turned red. At the end of the session,

Goodwin echoed Kessler's comments with a shrug. "Look at Kellerman's performance. Numbers don't lie." Then he sighed.

A phone call came through for Kurt at his office one afternoon. It was Frankie Evans's wife. Frankie had just checked in to a mental hospital. He'd had a "nervous breakdown." Jimmy Goodwin had been putting so much pressure on Frankie that he couldn't take it anymore. Kurt went to visit him. He discovered one of Jimmy's "girls" had wanted to date Frankie. When Frankie refused, things started happening at work. Frankie's performance reviews started being unacceptable. His budget was cut. His production goals dramatically increased. There had been several internal audits of his branch, even though everything was in order. Frankie cracked under the pressure. Eventually, he was given a disability retirement. This confirmed Kurt's attitude toward the bank.

Kurt didn't allow Art Kessler's praises to go to his head. He knew things were going to become unbearable at the bank. While he continued to work diligently, he looked for other possibilities. Although the situation at the bank was deteriorating, things seemed to get better with his family. Meghan was faithful, he adored his children, and his relationship with his parents had improved over the years. Kurt did his best to forgive some of the things his parents had said and done in the past. They loved him, and he loved them.

A Series of Unexpected Revelations

His father's health had declined over the past few years. He had suffered from a series of heart attacks. The first time, he had bypass surgery. The second time, angioplasty, and after the third heart attack, he had an atherectomy.

Mr. Kellerman's health deteriorated. He enjoyed nothing more than talking with Kurt, John, or James. Finally, after a fourth heart attack, he died in the intensive care unit at the hospital. Kurt grieved the passing of his father. The heart attacks had been spread out over more than fourteen years. During that period, his father had become a pillar Kurt trusted.

After his father's death, Kurt helped his mother dispose of many of his father's items. While searching through things, Kurt went through the old chest of drawers where he'd left all the letters he had received from Mary years ago. He'd read them one last time the week before his marriage, hid them away, and left them behind. As he looked through the chest, he discovered the letters were no longer there. He asked his mother about them.

Mrs. Kellerman said, "I suppose we need to talk about some things."

Kurt had an uneasy feeling about this. "I'm not sure I will like this, but go ahead and tell me." He braced himself for whatever was coming. Kurt told himself to keep control of his emotions and listen.

His mother spoke at last. "I hate to tell you, but we threw Mary's letters to you away when we came across them one day. You were married, and we didn't think you had any business having love letters from a former girlfriend lying around."

Kurt didn't say anything. There was a long, awkward pause. He held his tongue and waited to see if she would continue.

"I guess you know that we didn't want you and Mary to get married. She was a sweet girl, and we liked her very much. We knew you were head over heels about her, but it scared us to death."

Kurt felt his chest and throat tighten. It was hard to breathe. *They've lied to me. How many lies have they told? Will I ever know all of it?* "Why? What objections could you have had about Mary?"

"Well, you know your sister married a Roman Catholic several years before you started dating Mary. After they were married, your sister dropped out of church and became downright hostile to our beliefs. This was all because we allowed her to marry a Catholic. Mary was Catholic. We weren't going to make the same mistake twice. We had to let you go see her at Christmas, but we determined not to let you see her in Indianapolis again. We figured you would get over her and start dating other girls. She was hundreds of miles away. We limited your telephone calls and thought she would give up on you too. But it didn't work. Finally, when prom came, we pushed you into the date with Jacquie and figured that would do the trick. But you kept writing her."

"Was this something you did, or did Dad participate too? Also, what about the fact that I kept writing Mary?"

Tears sprung from his mother's eyes now. "Well, we didn't mail your letters to her. When you left them to mail, we threw them in the trash. She never received any of those. There may have been a couple of letters from her right after prom, and your father destroyed them too. I'm not sure about that. We were pretty sure the package that came in August was to break up with you, so we took a chance and let you have that. Then it was done. We did it because we loved you and didn't want you to end up like your sister."

I feel sick. This is a nightmare. How could they do that to me? To Mary. Judy was never serious about church. It had nothing to do with Jerry. I don't know if I can ever speak to Mom again. It was obvious Judy didn't want to go to church long before she met Jerry. But I want to hear everything right now. I want to know what happened!

"I can't believe you did that! I knew you were trying to push us apart, but I never dreamed you would steal our mail! Your ban on phone calls didn't work anyway. I spent hundreds of dollars calling her on a pay phone. And I want you to know something. Mary and I talked about our faith. She was planning to convert after we were married. She understood how important it was to me, you, and Dad. She loved you guys, and you treated her like she was something filthy! Don't you realize that Judy never intended to go to church or worship God the moment she left your house? She didn't go to church when she went away to school. Or when she got those summer jobs away from home. Her husband never went to church. They were two nonbelievers who didn't care about that stuff. I knew you did some of these things. But I never dreamed you did all of this. It explains so much I'd always wondered about. But what you did was wrong! It was wrong to do those things to me. It was wrong to do those things to Mary! It was evil. I'm sorry, Mom, but what you did was evil!"

Mrs. Kellerman was wringing her hands. Her mouth dropped open, and she was crying. Her eyes were red.

"But Meghan is a wonderful girl. We love her, and she's made you a wonderful wife. You have a wonderful family. We did it all for you. We did it because we love you."

Tears streamed down Kurt's face. He tried to take deep breaths to calm down. When he spoke, his voice was calm but firm. "Mom, you're right. Meghan is a wonderful girl. But I don't love her the way I love Mary. I've been heartbroken ever since the Thursday night before my prom. I hate myself because I allowed you to manipulate me into that. I love you and Dad because I am supposed to honor my parents, and I know you thought you were doing what was right. But you couldn't have been more wrong. It will take a while to get over all of this."

Kurt stood and paced back and forth across the room. He sighed half a dozen times. Next, he went to the sink and splashed cold water on his face. He dried off and sat down again. His eyes were red. His lips were drawn tight. He resumed speaking in a quiet, firm voice.

"As bad as what you did to me was, what you did to poor Mary was unspeakable. A seventeen-year-old girl whose father had died in a farm accident, whose mother was sickly and whom Mary had to be the caretaker for instead of her mother being there for Mary—who had to move to a large city and leave all her friends behind, including the boy she was going to marry—

and you lied to her, stole her mail, made her even more lonely than she was, and made me betray her. I don't know if I can forgive you for all that. I don't know if you *should* be forgiven for all of that. It's hard for me to take it all in that my parents, who I love and who I always looked up to as model Christians, could have been so cruel, so devious, so dishonest, so—I don't even know how to describe it."

Both were in tears. Kurt was furious. He wanted to strike out and wound someone. But he couldn't say or do anything more to his mother. He stood and paced again. He wanted to get in his car and drive it into a tree. He resisted the impulse. Kurt felt shock, disappointment, anger, nausea, and a thousand other emotions. He wept for Mary and how she had been treated. He was angry at himself for being obedient to his parents. He should have rebelled. How could he have ever allowed them to do that to him? To Mary? It felt as though he might burst from within.

His mother said, "What about Meghan? She's your wife. Don't do anything foolish."

"Apparently, I have a higher view of marriage than you or Dad have had. I won't leave Meghan. I won't divorce her if that's what you're worried about. Besides, Mary has a husband. Heaven only knows if she's happy. But I'm not going to chase another man's wife. I hope you understand that you broke the hearts of two people doing their best to live according to the values you claim to follow. Now that I think of it, the best thing I could've done my senior year would've been to not be a good boy and ask Mary not to be a good girl. If I'd gotten her pregnant, you would have been all for us getting married. Her family would never have allowed her to get an abortion! Then we'd all have been happy."

"Don't say that."

"But it's true! Because we tried to do what was right, you and Dad lied, cheated, and stole from us. Trying to obey and honor God made us vulnerable to what you did to us. If we'd done what was wrong, you would have welcomed her into the family. I can't talk about this anymore. I've got to do something to calm down, and then I've got to get out of here!" He left the house, got into his car, and took a long time to get home.

Things continued as usual, although Meghan noticed that Kurt was very moody. He never spoke to her about these things. How could he? Also, Kurt did not want to hurt Meghan. She'd saved his life years ago. Given him three wonderful children. He kept reminding himself of all the things she'd done for him. In addition, Kurt remembered his wedding vows and the biblical teachings on marriage. His life was built on obedience to God. He couldn't choose to disobey God just because someone had tricked him. It was not God's fault Kurt had been weak. That Kurt honored his parents even though they betrayed him.

Yet Kurt was consumed with guilt. He had betrayed Mary under pressure from his parents. He also felt he had betrayed Meghan by marrying her when he was in love with Mary. To make it all worse, Mary invaded his thoughts and dreams day and night. There was never a day that he was not consumed with her. Everything in his life was proof of his failure and disobedience to God. It was overwhelming.

Time passed, and the shock of that day lessened. The next time he saw his mother, she apologized in tears. It appeared she had no idea until she confessed her actions to Kurt just how much she had hurt him. She'd never even considered the pain her actions caused Mary. She was trying to protect her son, however misguided she may have been. Kurt accepted her apology, and they began to rebuild their relationship. But it would take time for him to work through what had happened.

Kurt continued trying to move past all of this and focus on the life he had built with Meghan. No matter what he did, somehow Mary would come into his head from nowhere. It was impossible to move past her.

One day, as Kurt had lunch, he bumped into an old acquaintance from back home, Marilyn Perkins. She'd been in the band in high school. She had moved here and worked as a receptionist for Kurt's doctor. Kurt invited her to sit with him. As they chatted, Marilyn said, "I heard something interesting about you last weekend."

Kurt raised his eyebrows. "What?"

"Well, I was at a family get-together. Mary Johnson was there. I don't know if you were aware of it, but she's a first cousin of mine. As we were talking, she mentioned you."

Marilyn paused to see if there was any reaction. Kurt could feel his pulse quicken. He wouldn't show his agitation. He decided to keep quiet and wait. It was apparent that Marilyn was enjoying herself.

She resumed. "Mary said that had she not moved to Indianapolis, you would have married. It surprised me. She seemed sad. I was just curious if that was true or something she just made up."

"We dated for nearly a year. I suppose we would have gotten married. With her in Indianapolis, it was difficult to manage a long-distance relationship, and things fell apart."

"Mary seemed very definite about it. She knew I saw you occasionally and asked how you were doing and what you were up to these days. She talked about you for quite some time."

My question is answered. Mary did love me. She wanted to marry me. Even now, she still cares about me. All these years, I've been right. We belong together. But what can I do? I feel sick, but I can't let Marilyn see that.

"Well, thanks for the information. I appreciate it. That was all true. Is she still married?"

"Yes, she is. But I don't think she's happy."

"I hate that for her. I wish that she was happy. She's a very nice person who deserves some happiness in her life. I need to get back to work now, but it was nice talking to you."

As he walked out of the diner, Kurt's mind raced. He wanted to get away as quickly as he could. Marilyn was a big gossip and would love to start something. At the same time, this was the first real news of Mary that Kurt had heard in years. He'd often wondered whether his feelings toward Mary were something he imagined or were real. He'd always told himself that Mary loved him and they had been ripped apart by a combination of fate and their parents. But sometimes, he asked himself whether Mary ever even thought of him. Maybe she was in love with this other guy and happily married. Maybe Kurt was just a faint memory that rarely, if ever, crossed her mind. He sometimes wondered if he just idealized Mary because of the shortcomings in his own life and marriage. He couldn't discuss these things with anyone, except perhaps Chuck Davis.

Kurt returned to the bank and threw himself into work for the rest of the day. Every time he finished a task or took a break, the lunch conversation haunted him. Mary agreed they would have married and wanted to know how Kurt was and what he was doing. Kurt would have loved to ask for more details, but it would have been wrong. *I need to get this out of my head and focus on something else.*

After a few sleepless nights, he was able to get back on track and refocus. But anytime he let his guard down, he was over-whelmed by that conversation and what Mary was thinking and doing. It seemed that no matter how hard he tried, something from out of his past with Mary came back to haunt him every so often. There was no peace of mind. There was sadness, guilt, and a sense of loss in which he felt he was drowning.

He got a chance to talk to Chuck about it. Kurt rambled on for an hour or more. Just saying it out loud was a relief to his fevered mind. There was at least an easing of pressure.

"So you've been right all these years despite what everyone else said. I'm sorry. That sounds hard. You know you can always talk to me. You're my best friend." Again, Kurt tried to move on with his life.

The kids were getting older. John neared graduation from high school. James started high school. Jennifer was in middle school. Meghan was still busy running after them, taking care of the house, and volunteering at church and school. Kurt tried to focus on the many blessings in his life.

During this period, Kurt grew more and more disillusioned with the bank. He'd taken several night classes, some online, and received a bachelor of arts in history. He contacted Dr. Darcy to see if the offer to provide a letter of recommendation for graduate school was still available. Kurt was a little surprised when Dr. Darcy responded. He still remembered Kurt and would provide the letter. Kurt planned to pursue a master's degree at a university about forty miles away. Dr. Darcy assisted him in getting admitted to the program.

Kurt's oldest son graduated from high school and received several scholarships to Northwestern University. James and Jennifer were doing well in school too. Even though Kurt was unhappy at the bank, he was still getting good annual reviews. The last training session for all the managers included advice from an attorney on hiding financial assets from your spouse. Kurt was offended by it. He wanted to get out.

Decisions, Decisions

Unhappy at home and unhappy at work, Kurt had an opportunity to change his situation. He had earned a master of arts in history. A nearby community college had an opening for a history instructor, and Kurt applied for the position. He received an interview, which seemed to go well. After a few weeks, he received a call and was offered the position.

Meghan voiced some concerns. "I know you don't like the bank. But you've been there a long time. It's safe and secure. Do you want to give that up? How long will it take you to be tenured? I would think they could always get new history teachers."

"The bank isn't as secure as you think it is. I look for the axe to fall any day now. The college wants someone local who will stay and help the program grow. I think I'd be safer there than at the bank."

"What about the pay? It's less than you make now. John's in college, and James will be in a few years."

"The starting pay is lower, but the ceiling is much higher. Remember, I've only received minimum raises since Mr. Goodwin took over. By the third year, I'll be making more. Plus, the insurance is less expensive but a better plan."

"It sounds like your mind is made up. I hope you know what you're doing."

A few weeks later, Kurt made an appointment to see Mr. Wiggins. It was set for Thursday. Kurt walked in and handed a letter of resignation to Mr. Wiggins. "I'm leaving the bank. I appreciate my time at the bank, but I've always wanted to teach history at the college level. I have the opportunity to do it now. It's a dream come true."

Mr. Wiggins accepted the letter and shook his hand. "I hate to see you leave, but who am I to stand between a man and his dreams? The number one thing I want from my managers is personal loyalty. A fellow who wants to do something else can't give that. Good luck. Thanks for dropping by."

Kurt started preparing for his new job. He would be responsible for introductory courses in American and European history. This would involve teaching five classes per semester. During his first year, he would do three classes in American History from 1607 until 1865 and two classes in European History from 1492 to 1792. Kurt was excited about it. *I wonder whether I can get the students' interest and be effective.* He had dreamed about this for years and couldn't wait to start. At the same time, he sometimes had a sick feeling in the pit of his stomach. The head of the department had already set the course syllabus. In future years, he would be able to tweak it, but the dean and the history department chairman were very definite that he was to adhere to the syllabus being used in the class.

The semester started, and all of Kurt's classes were full. He walked into his first class and handled many start-of-semester administrative duties. Then it was time to begin teaching. Of the forty students in the class, four or five were excited to study history, and another ten to fifteen were good students who didn't care. Half the class had no interest in American history but took it as a required class. They would put forth the minimum effort needed to pass, and that was all. This was going to be a challenge. Still, Kurt looked forward to it. Most of his classes, whether larger or smaller, had a similar makeup of students. His mind was already working on how to engage marginal students.

Over time, Kurt managed to increase the voluntary efforts of most of his students. There were always a few who were unreachable, but many students seemed to like Kurt and worked hard to do well in History 101 and History 111. His performance review went well. Things looked up as far as work was concerned.

A big scandal erupted at the bank after Christmas. Jimmy Goodwin was terminated as the bank president. He had been involved in a scheme to embezzle a lot of money. Several branch managers were found to be complicit in the plot. The bank board had to clean house. It was the biggest scandal in Kurt's hometown in thirty years. *I am so glad I got out of there before this happened.* With all the ethical problems Jimmy Goodwin presented, none of this was a surprise. The people Jimmy favored and who appeared to be his closest friends were the first to get charged with criminal activity. Jimmy had set them up as fall guys. The bank examiners and prosecutors would still get evidence that Jimmy was the ringleader, and he spent time in prison.

After a few years had passed, Kurt worked on his PhD in history. He enjoyed the research. It didn't feel like work to him. Things at the community college were going well. Occasionally, he was allowed to teach an extra course he designed, focusing on a particular aspect or era of history. After Kurt graduated with his PhD, he had the opportunity to teach at a small liberal arts college about an hour away.

He and Meghan packed up and moved. It was hard on Meghan as she had no friends in the new community, while Kurt could make friends through work. After about six months, they found a church they liked, which helped Meghan adjust. Meghan hated moving. She felt like she had no real home. Over time, she had become increasingly reluctant to get out and meet people. She went to a psychologist for a while but felt it didn't help her. Kurt tried not to think about it. But a question kept nagging at his mind. *Would Mary have handled all the changes better? I'll never know.*

Unexpected News

Kurt cleaned the gutters of his house on a Saturday afternoon. When he stretched to reach a little further to his right, the ladder fell. He fell around twelve feet before hitting the ground. Kurt landed on his side. It hurt like thunder. He still managed to finish cleaning the gutters. Kurt decided to ice his side and put some elastic bandages around his chest that night.

Meghan looked at Kurt and his home remedies. "You need to go to the emergency room."

"No. It's either bruised or cracked ribs. They can't do anything for that except what I've done."

"You're not a doctor. They probably should get X-rays and make sure."

"I've done this before when I played football. It feels the same. I know how to care for it."

On Monday, Meghan made an appointment for Kurt with their family doctor. Then she called Kurt to let him know. She'd found over the years that Kurt was stubborn about going to the doctor. This was the easiest way to get him there. Kurt grumbled but agreed to keep the appointment.

The doctor ordered X-rays and found that Kurt had three cracked ribs. The recommended treatment was to ice them and wrap them with an elastic bandage. Kurt laughed when he heard that. He was looking forward to saying "I told you so" to Meghan. He checked out at the reception desk before he left.

As Kurt was getting ready to leave, Marilyn Perkins, the receptionist, said, "I heard a lot about you last weekend."

"What did you hear?"

"I saw Mary Johnson this weekend. She mentioned you. She's done that before. Mary claims you guys would have married one another if she hadn't moved away. She also asked if I'd seen you in a while and wondered how you were doing. Mary is divorced now. Her ex was cheating on her, and she caught him. She's having a pretty rough time."

It was as though Kurt had been awakened from a long slumber. His pulse quickened. His senses were alert. He tried to master himself, although he was afraid it was obvious this hit him like a bolt of lightning. *Mary is free. She's no longer married. She wants to know about me. It's finally happening. I can be with Mary!* All this went through his mind in a flash. Then it felt like someone dumped a cooler of ice water on him. *She asked if I'm still married. I am. Meghan has never been unfaithful. I don't know how I could leave her. I gave my vows.* All of this happened in two or three seconds.

"I hate that. She was one of the nicest people I've ever known. I hope that things get better for her. I need to get going." *This is déjà vu all over again.*

Marilyn slipped him a card with his next appointment. "It

was nice to see you. I hope you get to feeling better." Kurt headed toward the exit.

He looked at the appointment card. It had the time and date of his follow-up. He flipped it over as he put it in his wallet. On the back of the card, in Marilyn's handwriting, were the words Mary Johnson Brown, followed by an address and telephone number. He stopped. Then he put the card in the back of his wallet. Kurt walked out to his car, got in, and took off. He went for a drive as he tried to sort out this information. It had been around six years since Marilyn had talked to Kurt about Mary. Now Mary was divorced and still asked about him. He had Mary's contact information for the first time in twenty-five years.

As Kurt drove off in the car, a million thoughts flooded his mind. Should he throw it in the trash? Call her? Write her a letter? She now lived about four hours away. Maybe he could see her. Perhaps he should forget it. What if Meghan found out? What would it do to his wife and children if it was discovered he was contacting Mary? But he wasn't planning on doing anything. Mary might not want to ever speak to him again. She made that clear the last time they spoke. But what if she did? Would he want to leave Meghan and finally have the girl of his dreams? But who was to say things would be all right between him and Mary? They hadn't spoken to one another in twenty-five years. Kurt knew that he had changed. He wondered how Mary had changed. The thoughts and questions in his head went on without end.

He turned the car toward home. He was exhausted. Kurt mused about how tired he felt. It seemed odd that emotional stress produced physical stress. After a short drive with his mind running wild, his body felt as if he had run a marathon. His ribs hurt, but there was more. The emotional strain was taking up every ounce of energy he had. Perhaps that was good. If Meghan thought Kurt acted tired and odd, she would attribute it to the cracked ribs. That took a load off his mind. Kurt got out of his car and went into the house.

It seemed almost impossible for Kurt to focus on anything. He would take the card out of his wallet and look at it a dozen times every day. There were no answers. He knew that he was risking injuring, even destroying, his wife and children, and himself, if he pursued Mary. At the same time, they'd never really had any closure. He more than ever believed that Mary had still been hurting and only wanted to wound him when she said she was in love with someone else and made him promise not to call anymore.

Some days he was busy enough that he was able to put it on the back burner of his mind. On other days it consumed him. He felt like he was on an endless roller coaster going nowhere. Kurt was paralyzed. He couldn't contact Mary, but he couldn't forget her either. She was always there. Now she was there more than she had been in years. Mary wasn't married. She wasn't someone else's wife. But Kurt was married. He was another woman's husband. He wrestled night and day with his dilemma. How could he look himself in the mirror if he reneged on the promises he had made at his wedding? Had he already done so just by thinking about Mary? Kurt was no longer sure he knew the difference between right and wrong.

Chapter 13
The Thunderbolt

Trying to Make Sense of a Crashing World

K urt needed to drive to Chicago to take care of some things for John a few weeks later. It was October 12, 2002. He made up his mind he would call Mary while in the car. That way he would be alone, with no real chance of interruption. Even as Kurt left town, he questioned whether he would make the call.

Will I call? Is it wrong for me to call Mary? If I don't call today, I never will. I want to call her. She must want to hear from me. I just don't know.

After an hour of driving time, Kurt punched the number on his cell phone. Every muscle in his body tensed as he heard the phone begin to ring. His mouth was so dry that Kurt wasn't sure he could even talk if Mary did answer the phone. On the fourth ring, a voice answered. Even after twenty-five years, Kurt recognized it.

"Hello," came Mary's voice on the other end of the line.

"Hello, Mary. This is Kurt. Would you please talk to me for a while? Please?"

"Yes. If you'll answer a few questions first," was the response. "Why are you calling me now? After all this time?"

"Because I just got your number a few weeks ago. I found out you were no longer married. I promised I wouldn't call you again when you told me you were in love with someone else. But that's changed now. You're no longer married to him. So I felt it wouldn't be breaking my promise if I called now. I hope that's all right."

"But why right now? Has anything happened?"

"Three reasons. First, for the first time in over twenty years, I discovered you are no longer married. Second, I got your phone number two weeks ago. Third, I knew that if you answered and would speak to me today, I could talk as long as you were willing without worrying about interruptions."

"Why won't you be interrupted? What are you doing?"

"I'm driving up to Chicago by myself. I have a five-hour drive, and no one can interrupt me. I can focus on talking to you. If you're willing to talk to me."

"Okay. How did you get my number? It's unlisted."

"Your cousin, Marilyn Perkins, gave it to me. She's the receptionist for the doctor I see. I fell and cracked a few ribs two weeks ago, and she talked to me and gave me your phone number."

"How many girls did you date that summer after you decided you should be free to date other girls?"

"None. There was no one I wanted to date except you. I didn't go out with anyone else until several months after you told me you were in love with someone else."

"Are you still married?"

"Yes."

"To the McGill girl?" Her voice was filled with disdain.

"Yes. I'm still married to her. I married her nearly three years after you got married and have been married to her ever since."

"Three years after I got married!? What are you talking

about? You got married in the summer of 1980! I didn't get married until a year later!"

"What do you mean?" Kurt ran onto the shoulder and jerked his car back on the road. He turned the volume up on his phone to ensure he heard everything correctly. "Your mother sent me a letter in 1977, returning some things. She said you were married, and she'd found some things of mine that you'd left behind after you moved out. She told me she'd realized I was a nice boy after all and wished me well. But mainly, she told me you were married and no longer lived with her and Bob."

"No! You got married on June 14, 1980. I waited a year after that before I got married."

"Yes. I got married June 14, 1980."

"Worst day of my life."

"But your mom sent me that letter. You were already married. And six months later, Tracker stopped by your house, hoping to see you. She told him that you were married. Besides that, I saw Lori in August of 1978, and she told me you were married. She went on and on about how nice your wedding was."

Mary whispered, "They must have lied. Mom and Lori lied to you. I wasn't married. I didn't know anyone had told you that. I thought you loved me. I loved you. I didn't marry until I saw in the hometown newspaper that you had married, and Marilyn confirmed it for me."

Kurt shook. His throat was tight. He pulled over to the side of the road. Tears blinded him.

"I would never have married anyone else if I'd known you were single. You'd told me you loved someone else. Your mother told me you were married. She told Tracker you were. Lori told me you were married on a couple of occasions. I don't know what to say. I couldn't marry anyone so long as there was even the tiniest hope that I could marry you. They crushed any hope that I had."

"I know Mom and Lori didn't want me to marry you. But I didn't think they would lie to stop it." After a moment of silence, she continued. "Why did you quit writing and leave me abandoned and all alone?"

"I didn't quit writing." Kurt explained what had happened. His parents, and possibly her mother, destroyed his letters. "When I called, you refused to talk to me."

"I didn't refuse to talk to you on the phone," she said.

"Your mother answered the phone several times and told me you didn't want to talk to me and I should leave you alone. The only times I got through to you were when you wrote about going to the Eagles concert and after I got to the university. Then I sent the roses. After the roses, I spoke to you several times. I sent another bouquet of roses, but you wouldn't talk. Then came New Year's Eve."

"Those were the only times I even knew that you called. I only received one bouquet. I was heartbroken. I couldn't believe you had just completely cut me off. I was angry with you. I wanted to hurt you. You hurt me so badly I felt I would die."

"I'm so sorry for the mistakes I made. It was all my fault. I let you down. I could make excuses, but it can't change anything. I know I was arrogant back then. I thought I could work things out. I never dreamed you wouldn't take me back. For whatever it's worth, I've been humbled. A broken heart can do that. You have the prettiest smile, the sweetest face, and the most beautiful eyes I've ever seen. I would give anything if I could change all the ways I failed you."

"Thank you. I'm sorry too."

It was difficult for Kurt to grasp this new information. He said, "So I only got married after I was convinced you were married to someone else. You only got married when you knew I was married to someone else. I'm so sorry I believed them. I don't know how to apologize for all the mistakes I made. You know that I will love you until the day I die. I've never stopped loving you."

"I was crushed when you got married. I didn't realize you wouldn't ever call again because I made you promise. I just wanted to make you suffer like I had."

"I realize that. I've often wondered about it. But I'd hurt you so many times already that I felt I had to keep my promise. I'll never forget the look on your face when you took my hand off your arm that night. The one person I've never wanted to let down or hurt in any way is the one person that I've most injured. Please forgive me, Mary."

"We were too young to deal with everything they did to us," said Mary softly. "I know you didn't mean to hurt me."

Kurt's heart pounded. "If I were to come down your way in a few weeks, would you be willing to meet me for lunch? It's not a date. I would like to talk to you face-to-face. There is so much we didn't know. My parents and your mother both did all sorts of things to break us apart. I was too obedient and, I suppose, too immature to disobey them. I'm so sorry."

Mary thought for a moment.

"Not as long as you're married. If you are ever single, I would be happy to see you. We could do it anywhere or anytime, but not while you're married."

"I understand. That makes sense. I want you to know that you are in my thoughts every day and have been since the first time we went out and always will be. I pray for you each day and will continue to do so. I won't call or write you again unless I'm single. If you ever need to call, write, or contact me in any way, please do it. I suppose it doesn't make any difference, but I always have and always will love you."

"I've always loved you too. But you're married. I guess it's time to say goodbye."

"I guess so. If you want to talk a little about anything, I'll be glad to talk before we hang up. It's great just hearing your voice."

"Mom decided you were a nice boy after all." Mary laughed a little. "You're the only person I've ever dated that she said that about. Of course, she waited until she knew she'd broken us up."

They did discuss a few other things. After nearly an hour, they said goodbye and hung up. Kurt got back onto the road and continued his trip. His head was spinning. Neither he nor Mary had realized some of the things their families had done to keep them apart. Mary's moral compass impressed Kurt. She wouldn't see him if he was married. Once more, a million thoughts and questions filled his mind. He really couldn't think straight. Kurt spent the night in Chicago with John. The next day, he headed back home.

What to Do

The phone call had yielded a lot of information for Kurt to absorb. His parents had betrayed him. Mary's family had lied to them both and betrayed her. Kurt knew he would never have married Meghan if there had been the tiniest hope of ever working things out with Mary. But that was more than twenty years ago. Was he going through a midlife crisis? No. That wasn't it. His romantic feelings had always been for Mary. There was no question about that. It wasn't that his feelings for Meghan had ever been what they were for Mary. He'd married Meghan after all hope was gone.

He had married Meghan. They had three children together. Kurt had shared wedding vows with Meghan. He couldn't take them back. Some people tried. But Kurt knew that would be wrong. His marriage was in trouble. *Part of it was his fault. Part of it was Meghan's fault. She knew I'd been troubled over Mary. Our courtship and marriage weren't romantic. Still, that was my fault. She accepted me in good faith. But what was right? What was wrong?*

Mary's words kept coming back to Kurt. "We were too young to deal with everything they did to us." As usual, Mary was so wise. Everything she said was right. Her wisdom, her courage, and her moral values were some of the things that Kurt had fallen in love with twenty-seven years ago. These, along with her beauty and kindness, were why he bought an engagement ring for her in December 1975. Why? Why hadn't he given it to her? She said she loved someone else. But just to hurt him. He knew he deserved it. Kurt knew that he was guilty of allowing his parents to control his actions even when obeying them resulted in terrible cruelty to Mary.

Kurt began to contemplate divorce. If he chose that route, it was against everything he had ever believed and stood for. On the other hand, Mary was worth it. He could walk away from a lot if Mary was at the end of the road. He discussed it with Chuck, who was shocked that he would even consider it. Chuck was kind and sympathetic.

"You've struggled with your love for Mary since we became friends. I know it's hard. But I know what you believe and what the Bible says. You don't have any grounds for divorce."

"But it was so wrong! So unfair. I hurt Mary, and I can make it right with her."

"Yes. But the only way to make it right with Mary is to be wrong, unfair, and hurt Meghan and the kids. You can't undo what you did to Mary. You shouldn't do the same thing to Meghan and your children."

Kurt knew Chuck was right. He just wished he wasn't.

Next, Kurt went to a marriage counselor. He shared a lot, but not all, of his story. The counselor was a Christian. He pointed out what appeared to be a successful marriage, career, family, and his religious beliefs. Kurt told him that he struggled with whether to walk away from those beliefs for the first time in his life.

"You realize if you leave your wife, she will be crushed. It would hurt her emotionally, financially, and spiritually. It would be entirely your fault."

"I know. But I love Mary."

"Then what about your children? Especially your daughter. She's just starting her teen years. Statistically, this is when a divorce would be most destructive to her. Are you willing to take responsibility for that? It would also hurt your sons but likely ruin your daughter's life."

"I wouldn't want to do that. But it's so hard. I don't know how I can walk away from Mary."

"Maybe that wouldn't be as difficult if we worked on your relationship with Meghan. If you improve your relationship with her, it will help break your bond with Mary. Why don't we talk about that? What can we do to make you happier in your marriage?"

Kurt cut him off. "No! I got just what I asked for out of my marriage. Both the good and the bad are close to what I expected. I'm not interested in that. Meghan has no interest in changing, and I've no right to ask her to change. Talking about it would only build resentment. My marriage is tolerable. That's what I presumed it would be."

"That's setting the bar low. That will never lead to happiness. Just more frustration and depression."

"If happiness is the goal, then I'll get a divorce and do whatever it takes to make things right with Mary. Even if I fail, I'll be happier failing with Mary than succeeding with Meghan."

The counselor threw his hands into the air and sighed. "If that's how you feel, I can't help you. Just get out of here. We're finished."

No one could make this decision for Kurt. He hoped someone would tell him that he should divorce Meghan and chase after Mary. But the only people who told him what he wanted to hear were people with a different view of marriage, the Bible, Christianity, and morality than Kurt. His choices boiled down to being true to his beliefs or not. Kurt had never realized that what had always appeared to be a simple choice could be so difficult when you were the one who had to make it.

Doing the Right Thing

Kurt had to decide. No one could do it for him. It would be one of the most difficult decisions of his life. There would be a great deal of pain whatever he chose. While it was apparent Mary still cared for him, there was no guarantee things would work out. He knew they had both changed. They both felt love for one another. He didn't know what everyday reality would be if he divorced and pursued Mary. Kurt's head ached. He was exhausted. Something had to give. He had to choose a direction and follow it. He had to choose, no matter how painful or disappointing it might be.

After weeks of soul-searching, Kurt came to a decision. He knew it would be wrong to divorce his wife and abandon his children, even though his passion, his infatuation, and his love for Mary might crush him. He wanted to take a chance and go to Mary. It was his fondest wish, the greatest desire of his life. But there would be no happy ending for his life. He would meet his obligations, keep his commitments, and live his life with honor. Even as he reasoned this out, Kurt knew his heart would always belong to Mary. For the rest of his life, he would inexplicably shed tears that no one else would understand. Kurt would bear the guilt for what he did to Mary. He would not add to that guilt by betraying Meghan, John, James, and Jennifer as well. Betraying them could not lead to anything good. Kurt once again wrote Mary.

My dearest and most beloved Mary,

I'm writing this with a broken heart. I've always loved you, and I always will, until the day I die. I apologize for all the pain I've caused you. I pray that you can forgive me. As I said, I never would have married if I hadn't been convinced you were already married. Your mother and sister lied to me. My parents lied to me. They prevented us from talking on the phone. They stole our mail. I don't know how we could have expected that. But I failed you. I've been brokenhearted ever since.

As much as I would love to divorce Meghan and leave my family, and I hope you would give me a second chance, I know it would be wrong to do so. The Bible is clear on that, and we both know it.

If for some reason I am ever single, I will do my best to win you back. But until that day, I must stay away. You have the most beautiful eyes and the prettiest smile, and you are the sweetest person I've ever known. I can't believe I let them take you away from me.

My heart forever belongs to you, and you alone,
Kurt

For months, Kurt was in a state of deep depression. Had he thrown away his last chance of happiness in life? Had he once again injured Mary? Was there any point in going on with life? All these questions rolled through his mind in a continuous refrain.

Life continued. Kurt finally knew the full story of what had happened to prevent his and Mary's marriage all those years ago. There were feelings of shame, guilt, pain, and at least some relief at finally knowing the truth. Kurt had always known that he was missing some information. The idea that he had been lied to about Mary being married had never been anything he suspected. Whether or not his parents had planned and worked together with Mary's mother and sister was the only thing he didn't know. He supposed it didn't matter at this point. Four people took it into their heads to shatter all of Kurt's and Mary's hopes and dreams. They had done it with devastating effectiveness. Kurt and Mary were still unhappy and suffering a quarter of a century later. The only comfort he took was that he had been right all along. Mary loved him, and he loved Mary. People could keep them apart, but they could not change that fact.

Kurt talked to Chuck several times over the next few months. At times Kurt despaired of his decision. He was as miserable as ever.

"It's just so hard. It would have been so easy a couple of months ago to leave it all behind and start fresh with Mary, assuming she would still have me. But this is just slogging through the mud one day at a time."

Chuck said, "Of course, it would be easy to leave Meghan. It's always easy to do the wrong thing. Doing what is right is hard. That's why so many people do the wrong thing, and so few choose to do what is right. You've chosen the hard way because it was the right thing to do."

This insight was so evident that Kurt had to stop and think about it. Chuck was right. Wrong things were so easy. Almost every bad thing he'd ever done was because it seemed like it would be easier than doing the right thing. Even though Mary would always be the love of his life, it would be wrong to mistreat Meghan and his children and break his vows and obligations to them. Even though it would not lead to happiness, abandoning them and breaking his word appeared to be the way to happiness. It would probably be filled with its sorrows.

Carrying On

Kurt had decided to continue with life, but he had other issues to address. Was it possible to improve his relationship with Meghan? He supposed he should try. Perhaps he should try to be more romantic. That was so easy with Mary, but not with Meghan. But Meghan was his wife.

He began surprising her with small tokens of affection and occasionally with flowers or candy. At first it seemed to help the relationship. However, the effect did not last. Meghan complained that he should spend the money on more practical things or save it. Kurt gave up on that approach. He tried a few other things to spark some romance in their relationship, but it all came to nothing.

Kurt did make a lifestyle change. In the past, he had dealt with stress by some physical activity. He would run, chop wood, or do exercises. Now, when Kurt was experiencing stress, he would eat. He had been ten to twenty pounds overweight for a few years, but now he gained even more. Kurt put on another fifty pounds and was very overweight.

Chuck asked Kurt about his weight gain. Chuck had always stayed in excellent shape. He was concerned about Kurt's health.

"Kurt, you've put on a lot of weight. Do you have a health problem? You know you can always talk to me."

"It was on purpose. I'd never let Mary see me this way. It's a way to protect my marriage. I can't make it through a single day without wanting to run away and find Mary."

Whatever Chuck expected, it wasn't this. "You're kidding! Don't you care about your health or how Meghan and other people see you?"

"Nope. They can take me or leave me. But I won't let Mary see this. It may be the only thing preventing me from doing something foolish."

John remained in Chicago. He had graduated from college, got a master's degree in business administration, and was working for a large firm. James had majored in chemical engineering and was employed in Fort Wayne, Indiana. Jennifer was attending a nearby university and studying psychology. Things were going well for the Kellerman family. It was difficult for Kurt and Meghan to adapt to being empty nesters. Their children were what they most shared in common. Without them at home, there was a bit of a strain on their relationship. They muddled through and visited their children as frequently as possible.

Kurt's mother's health had always seemed to be good. One night, Kurt called her, and she did not feel well. He drove over and brought her to spend the night with him and Meghan. The next morning, he took her to the emergency room. It took over a week to diagnose her as having ovarian cancer. She was in the hospital continuously for a little over a month before she passed away. On one of the last occasions that she and Kurt were alone, she apologized for what she and Kurt's father had done to him and Mary thirty years before. She had felt guilty about it for a long time. It did help bring a little healing to Kurt.

Jennifer got married to her high school sweetheart after graduating from college. He was a mechanical engineer. She went to grad school and received her master's degree after marriage. Around two years later, James was married. John didn't get married until his mid-thirties.

Kurt enjoyed his new position. It had been his lifelong dream. Both at the community college and now at the liberal arts college where he taught, he made history come alive to most of his students. His classes became some of the most popular on campus. It was very rewarding to him.

Jennifer and her husband wound up living only ten miles from Kurt and Meghan when her husband, Rich, got a promotion that caused them to relocate nearby. Kurt got to spend a lot of time with his grandchildren. From all outward appearances, it looked as though Kurt had lived the American dream.

Chapter 14
Till Tomorrow Isn't Coming

O nly Chuck, and possibly Mary, knew that each day was a struggle for Kurt. Repeatedly, he relived the precious moments he'd had with Mary. She haunted his dreams and was with him throughout the day. There was never more than a moment of respite from the thought of her. Every time he was in the car, she was leaning against him, his arm around her shoulder, stealing glances at the pretty smile, those beautiful piercing brown eyes, that sweetest of all persons he'd ever known.

The years continued to pass. Kurt enjoyed work. He and Meghan relished life together at times. At other times, Kurt seemed to withdraw into another world that was all his own and shut Meghan out.

Meghan had some issues with her parents. They were very controlling. They had been bitter ever since Meghan had moved away from her hometown. They tried to control Meghan's life to the extent they could. Her father passed away after Kurt took the position at the liberal arts college. But her mother continued to treat Meghan like a five-year-old until her dying day.

Kurt tried to comfort Meghan regarding her parents. He

suggested she see a psychologist, but Meghan wasn't interested. Strangely enough, Meghan's abusive parents made Kurt feel closer to her. Still, their love for one another—and Kurt did love Meghan—was never the deep, passionate love that he had for Mary until the day he died.

Life went on. Kurt got sick while on vacation one year. After going to several doctors over the following year, he was diagnosed with cancer. He took the treatments that were recommended, including seeing a psychologist. At times he showed signs of improvement. Meghan had hopes he would recover. Their friends prayed for Kurt's healing. But after two years, the treatments became ineffective. The cancer started to spread again. A new treatment was given. It was effective for nearly a year. The cancer then spread even more. Kurt was experiencing a great deal of pain. Meghan and his family wanted him to start a new type of treatment.

It would probably extend his life by six months. Kurt was tired. He loved his family, but the treatments were becoming more painful and less effective.

Kurt thought it over. The new treatment would, at best, extend his life another six months. His quality of life had deteriorated over the previous six months. Then Kurt began to reflect on his life. After thinking it over for about a week, Kurt decided not to continue with any new treatments.

His family tried to persuade him to change his mind, but Kurt refused. The more they asked him to reconsider, the more he embraced his decision. Kurt started thinking of things he wanted to accomplish in the little time he had left. He realized they would need to be done quickly, as without any treatments, he would be hindered in a short time.

He started working on a project. He did not know how he would ever get it delivered. But he must find someone who would accept responsibility for doing so and then act faithfully and respect his privacy.

Kurt began to write. He was writing to Mary. He needed to say goodbye to her one last time. Even if she no longer cared for him, he needed to let her know his feelings. So Kurt started writing.

Dearest Mary,

Who in a just and fair world would be named Mrs. Mary Elizabeth Kellerman. I am terminally ill and don't have much time left. It's been nearly twenty-five years since we last spoke. I need to tell you that I still love you. I always have and I will until my dying day. In my heart, I have always been faithful to you and you alone. I thank God for the days we had together. My only regret in life is that they did not last. But my love for you did last. It never wavered. I love you.

Do you remember that rainy Labor Day? September 2, 1974? We spent the afternoon in your house listening to records and making out, and for the first time in my life, I asked a girl to dance with me at something other than a school dance. The first song we ever danced to was "Till Tomorrow." It was on Don McLean's American Pie album. I've been waiting for fifty years to dance with you again. But thanks to our families, it never happened. I listen to that song almost daily, fantasizing that I'm dancing with you one more time. Our bodies pressed together, my arms around you, our cheeks touching, swaying to the music.

I've waited a lifetime to dance with you again. I now realize this song asks the question to the story of our lives. Why weren't we free to be lovers? I apologize again for any pain or sorrow I've ever given you. In my way, I've been as faithful to you as it is possible to be. I've never loved anyone as I loved you. But I now realize, with my health failing, that our dance to "Till Tomorrow" will never come. I've waited my entire lifetime for it. But now I realize it will not come. I hope and wish the very best for you. If you no longer feel any love for me, that's all right. I want you to know that every day of your life since our first date, there was one person who loved and adored you. I know I failed you. I throw myself on your mercy as my final days pass. May God bless you and keep you.

I've written a poem for you. It isn't very good. But I've said it repeatedly in my prayers, dreams, and silent moments for decades. I share it with you now.

Brown Eyes
Each day I bear the pain that only you and l can know.
Never leaving my side, never leaving your side,
On and on we go.
I awaken from dreams where we're together,
Knowing they will never be.
It's all my fault, though I left you alone,
I thought you'd come back to me.

Beautiful brown eyes, the prettiest smile,
And sweetest person that I have ever known.
You keep me awake every night
Throughout my days my thoughts are of you alone.

How could you possibly understand
The words you will never hear
You haunt my every moment,
So far away and yet so near.
I wrote a letter to give you freedom,
But it wasn't to say goodbye.
They lied, they stole, and tore us apart,
Leaving us both to cry.

Beautiful brown eyes, the prettiest smile,
And sweetest person that I have ever known.
You keep me awake every night
Throughout my days my thoughts are of you alone.

I'm driving and you appear beside me
I've failed, though I tried my best.

You're with me every moment.
Awake or asleep, without you I'll never rest.
But the most wonderful thing in my life
The thing that gave it meaning
Was knowing that we loved one another
Though our time together was fleeting.

Beautiful brown eyes, the prettiest smile,
And sweetest person that I have ever known.
You keep me awake every night
Throughout my days my thoughts are of you alone.

I don't know if that is any good, but it expresses exactly how I feel about you. I ask God's blessings on you and your children as the day of my leaving this world approaches.

There is one last request I ask of you. I have no right to do so. But I pray that you will. After reading this letter, if you still love me, would you listen to "Till Tomorrow" and remember, and in your heart, have one last dance with me?

Thank you,
With all my love, for you and you alone,
Kurt Kellerman

Kurt sealed the letter in an envelope. He tucked it away nearby. Chuck Davis dropped by to visit his friend.

"Hi Kurt, how are you feeling?"

"You know how it is. Let's talk about something important."

"Sure. You can tell me anything. What is it?"

"Chuck, you're my best friend. Please do one last thing for me. It's the most important favor I'll ever ask of you."

Chuck's eye twitched a little. He looked uncomfortable. "What is it?"

"You know everything about my life. We were best men for

one another. I've confided things to you that no one else knows. I have a sealed envelope here. Would you take it and promise that you will see that it finds its way to Mary Johnson? It's my goodbye to her. Please?"

The two friends' eyes welled up with tears. Chuck hugged his best friend. "Don't worry. I promise that Mary will get this. I'll hand it to her myself. I'll do it right away. No one else will ever know. I promise."

"You're the only person I could entrust with this. Thank you, my friend. God bless you."

Chuck took the envelope, gave Kurt another hug, and left.

Meghan and their children supported Kurt through his final days. Kurt tried to show his love and appreciation for them. He hoped in his heart that he had been faithful to God, Mary, Meghan, and his children. He seemed to have quit struggling each day. Kurt was no longer living in the past and dreaming of what might have been. Neither was he living in a future dream where he got what he wanted. He was living in the present, making the best of every day. No more anger or worries about who had betrayed him or Mary. He felt things had been set right with Mary, although his heart still broke for her. Their children surrounded Meghan. They would comfort her at his passing when Kurt was no longer there to comfort her.

A few hundred miles away, a letter lay on a table by a chair. Mary Johnson started her playlist entitled "Favorite Songs." She stood alone in her living room as "Till Tomorrow" began to play. With tears streaming down her cheeks, she swayed to the music, dancing in her heart with the only man she'd ever loved. Without knowing whether he had followed the right course, Kurt was ready for death. He looked forward to death as to the end of a very long day. Kurt faced his final days with peace in his heart and love for everyone.

Made in United States
Orlando, FL
16 October 2024

52778498R00133